THAT NAMELESS THING

Sandie Giustina

ISBN 978-1-63784-709-1 (paperback)
ISBN 978-1-63784-710-7 (digital)

Hawes & Jenkins Publishing
16427 N Scottsdale Road Suite 410
Scottsdale, AZ 85254
www.hawesjenkins.com

Printed in the United States of America

Dennis Keith Scott...

To whom each and every book is dedicated. He is my eternal inspiration; my eternal love; without whose touch on my life I would be... less than who I am. I would have missed the fulness of heart, the fulness of life and the fulness of love that he inspired.

When I heard your voice, all was well. When you were away, I was cloaked in a coat of lonliness, but my heart toward you is filled with gratitude because you made me alive. I was filled with joy to hear your laughter, to see you smile. My heart was full because you filled the empty spaces.

Michael Ladig...

Who proved to me that the heart lives on... inspite of the circumstances of life.

My children, grandchildren and great-grandchildren because... they are worthy.

To my parents who raised, loved, tollerated and survived all the hell this wild, stuborn girl, with this demanding immagination put them through.

Contents

Introduction from the Grand-daughter...

GROWING UP, I LEARNED A *lot about my grandmother, but I'm sure I don't know everything. Most of my life, I guess I was too young to notice. I think I started noticing more when I turned 18. That's when I became an adult, I guess you could say. I got pregnant and then I got married at 19; who would have thought that?*

Anyway, I appreciate her more now that I understand all the things she went through for me and my sister. I love to see her smile. None the less, I think of her as a strong and independent woman; someone I want to be someday. She works hard for what she wants and I think she deserves it all. So, to you grandma, I love you so very much. You are my hero. I do give thanks for all your wisely advice and all the things you have taught, done and given me.

I really couldn't ask for a more wonderful and beautiful grandmother cause you are the best. I love you.

Brandi Urback... the granddaughter

Prologue

Life that is not real… is wasted.
If we fill it with unrealizable dreams,
We fill it with shadows.
It is then a suspension, a postponement,
A shunning of reality.
If we call such hours real
We are killing life.
We smother and deny and banish it.
Then one day we have no life;
For we have let that which has no life for us
Steal the real life that could have been ours.

That Nameless Thing…

WHAT NAMELESS THING ARE WE *speaking of? Is it emotional… feelings that you experience, but you are not quite sure what they are. Is it love? Is it infatuation? Is it a crush? Vengence? Anger? Frustration? Or maybe something as simple as friendship?*

Or is that nameless thing some sort of monster, beast, creature that you cannot identify? Wild animals you are not familiar with? Werewolf as in fables; an unreal thing, but you have seen it? Is it an alien, a ghost, one from the past or future? Or maybe just a stranger who, when you look into his eyes, burrows deep inside you?

Or is that nameless thing a shadow; simply a shadow of an evil person; or a shadow of a dreadful creature so grotesque that to actually see it would be beyond what our minds can endure.

Or is that nameless thing a treasure, but you don't know why it is so precious or how it came to be? Is it a treasure as your eyes have seen it or did it become a treasure when you touched it to your skin? Did it somehow work its way into your heart to become a treasure?

Is it a shadow of your life experience that your mind is deterring, for to actually see it... admit it... it would be beyond what your mind could comprehend or endure?

Is it outside lurking in the dark, is it under your bed or down the hall, is it in those who surround you or is it in your head? Is it an atrocious reality or the conjuring of the mind or even the heart? Dare we even seek to discover... that nameless thing?

Chapter 1

"WELL RAIN, ARE YOU READY to begin?"

"I think so. I don't really have a choice. I need to talk to someone; my head is spinning out of control and everything is getting all jumbled up. I need clarity and I can't see it on my own."

"Good then, I'm glad you're here. I intend to help you if I can."

"You have to."

"Let's get started then. The form you filled out says you are here for several reasons... you bought a gun, but it only makes you more afraid."

"Yes."

"And you have concerns about your brother... correct?"

"Yes."

"And two of your sisters have died recently; I'm sorry for your loss. Which of your concerns are more prominent in your head? Where would you like to start?"

"I don't know; whatever you think would be easiest. I'm really nervous; I just want to run, but I need help. Sometimes I think I'm loosing my mind."

"Alright then, let's start with the gun. Tell me why you bought it and why you think it upsets you."

"My two sisters were murdered and my brother insisted I get a gun."

"Was the murderer caught? Does he think..."

"I don't know. My brother won't let me watch TV or read newspapers and he won't tell me anything. He just says he's taking care of it."

"Do you have other siblings?"

"Yes, there were 8 of us; 7 girls and my brother."

"Did he make the other girls get guns?"

"No. My sister Blaze caries a gun; always has, but he didn't seem concerned about the others having a gun or maybe he just didn't think they could handle it. Ironic huh? I'm the one who can't handle it."

A slight smile jerked at the corners of Echo McMaster's mouth as she jotted down a note. Echo had been a pyschiatrist for 19 years with an 89% success rate. She followed her patients lives for 5 years after the conclusion of their treatment. She considered that enough time to determine victory or failure. So far, only one failure had ended in death, but that was one too many. She couldn't let it happen again.

"Do you know how to use a gun? Have you practiced with it?"

"River told me what to buy and he showed me how to use it when I got home, but that's all."

"Then I want you to take lessons and practice, so you can get a permit for a concealed weapon. Once you do that you may feel more comfortable, but if not we can re-evaluate that then. I think moving on is more important at this time."

"Okay, I can't believe I didn't think of doing that myself."

"You've recently lost two of your siblings; your mind has enough to deal with right now. You're 34... is that correct?"

"Yes."

"How far back do your memories go?"

Rain sat in slience trying to concentrate. Echo waited.

"I don't know. Maybe when I started school."

"Tell me about your parents... what they were like, what they did for a living, their relationship with each other and your relationship with them. Don't stress over it; just say whatever comes to your mind."

"My mom, Bette, was small... 5'5". She was heavy set and always seemed old and sad. She didn't work. I always thought of her

as weak and strong. I know that doesn't make sense; a complete contridiction, but when my dad was around she was weak. When he was
gone or she could stay out of his way, she was strong. She never knew
we exhisted when he was around. She only took care of us when he
was out of sight. She hid her pregnancies cause he'd have beaten her
and she had the babies at home by herself... that was strong."

Rain felt like she should have tears, but there were none. She
had never known her sisters exhisted or were coming until they were
there.

"How did she hide being pregnant until she was full term?"

"She was pretty heavy and she always wore loose clothes. Being
small I guess, she didn't get all that big. I really don't know, but that's
what I always thought... that she was lucky she was fat."

"I see. What did your dad do when they were born."

"Nothing. He acted like they didn't exist. We had a big old
house and mama kept the babies away from him."

"Alright; what else can you tell me about your dad?"

"He was small too, 5'8"; stocky, not fat. He drove truck locally
here in town and as far as Clarkston and Oak City. He was home
every night by 6:30. He ate dinner, watched TV, drank 6 beers and
went to bed. Sometimes on the weekends his buddies came for poker
and mom slave served them; sometimes he'd go out drinking and
come home drunk. He'd force her to... you know, and he did it any-
where he wanted." Rain paused to compose herself and Echo waited
silently.

"Other times he'd just watch sports and drink. He yelled at me
a lot, but never at my sisters or brother. It was like they didn't exhist
for him. Every night my mother would take his abuse in silence and
then he'd pass out."

"And how did you feel about that?"

"I hated him. I don't think I ever thought of him as my father.
Just the drunk who lived there."

"And your mother?"

"Indifferent mostly. I loved her I think; because I thought of
her as a mother and that's what you do. I felt bad for her, but I knew

better than to interfere. She made sure I had food and clean clothes, but we didn't talk much or spend time together."

"Lets move on for now. Tell me about your brother." *Why did she seem so emotionless? Had she seperated herself from her parents reality to survive?* The girl never looked her in the eyes; she needed her to.

"River? What do you want to know?"

"What he was like, how you got along; were you close?"

"We don't do things together if that's what you mean, but he talks to me all the time; about my sisters mostly… sometimes about me."

"Does he share his life with you?"

"Oh god no. He never talks about himself. Well, except for one time he was trying to make me feel better about something; he used an example of himself. Our last name is "Hardecky" and this last name is no big deal to me or my sisters, but my brother took a lot of shit for it. From the time he was 8 or so, the kids would tease him and say things like, "*Hey… how hard is that little dinky of yours?*" It followed him in some fashion or another all through high school. It seemed like quite a stretch from decky to dinky, but… I guess to boys."

"Was he bitter about it? Were you being teased at the time? Is that why…?"

"No, he got angry at first I think, but then he just blew it off and avoided those people. I don't remember what he told me for, but I don't think I was ever teased… just ignored."

"What is your earliest memory of him?"

Rain sat in silence again, trying to remember; no thoughts came, but she felt pain… fear. She winced.

'Finally.' Echo thought… *'an emotion.'* "Rain, I'd like you to lie back and relax; close your eyes."

"Why?"

"You appear to be afraid of what ever you were thinking and it might be easier to talk about if you…"

"But I don't remember anything. I can't remember when I first thought of my brother."

4

"So you don't remember, but when you tried you felt pain and fear?"

"Sort of..."

"Has your brother ever hurt you?"

"You mean like hit me or something?"

"Yes."

"No, of course not. He is always soft and caring; protective of me."

"He never teased you or belittled you or hurt your feelings?"

"No, he's the only one in the whole world that I know loves me."

"Then let's take it in that direction. Lay back and close your eyes; relax. Think of the times he's protected you or comforted you. Just let your mind drift and speak whatever comes into your head."

15 minutes passed in silence. Echo was afraid they'd run out of time. She always allowed an extra hour for the first visit, just in case. Even so, there was only 30 minutes left. Another 10 minutes passed before the silence was broken and the words began to flow like a river.

"I was 4; I was watching cartoons and my dad came home early... he'd already been drinking. He yelled for my mom. *Bette.*" He said, *"Leave that shit smelling dinner and get in here. What the fuck is this girl doing watching my TV?"*

"I only let her watch the cartoons for an hour if it's raining, like today, and she can't go outside. Rain, turn that off and go to your room now." My mom said.

"No, let her stay. It's time she learned what her job will be when she gets to be ripe."

"My mom came out of the kitchen and the look on her face scared me. Her eyes were big and her mouth full-open, like she was shocked or scared and when she talked, her voice had a tremor. She said, *"Tom no! You can't make her watch that. She's just a baby. She's not ready."*

"Shut the fuck up bitch! Get over here!" He grabbed her arm and pulled her to him. I was scared and wanted to run, but I couldn't move. I couldn't stop staring at them. He pulled her skirt to the floor and said, *"Finally... you finally learned not to wear those fucking*

panties that make your pussy stink. A pussy has to breathe… it needs fresh air."

"I didn't know what he was talking about, but I knew my mama was scared and I thought he was going to hurt her somehow. I'd heard yelling and fighting and crying before… lots, but I'd never been there to see it. I was mostly outside or in my room. I was afraid I was going to cry and I knew if I did, my dad would walk away from my mom and come over and back-hand me. When he did that I usually flew back against whatever was behind me."

"Then he threw her back on the couch and for no reason he back-handed her across the face. I saw blood. He yelled at her again. *"You ugly fucking bitch, I can't stand to look at your face; turn over."* Then he grabbed her and turned her on her face. I remember thinking how mad he'd be when he saw the blood that would be on the couch from her face. It would be worse than when she forgot or didn't have time to clean up the food he'd dropped there."

She was barely stopping for breath, but Echo did not want to interrupt. Information on a traumatized childhood was usually very difficult to get, but it was flowing from her and the more she revealed the better the chance that she could help her. Remembering these details as a 4 year old was rare, but having them so alive and real within her after all these years, even more so.

Rain barely paused before continuing. "He pulled her butt up in the air and haulked up a big guber and spit on her. I gagged and struggled for control so as not to throw up… spit always makes me want to throw up. Then he pulled his pants down and I saw what a man looked like for the first time. He shoved it in her butt. She screamed. You could tell she was trying not to, but she couldn't stop herself. I guess it just hurt too much. I tried to look away, but it was like someone was holding my head and I couldn't turn it."

"Where was my brother?" I thought. I had seen some old shows on TV where there was an older brother who took care of their younger brother or sister; protected them. That's what I wanted. I closed my eyes tight and that's when I felt the hands on my shoulders. Then I heard his voice, *"Rain, come on; I have to get you out of here."*

"I opened my eyes and he was there. River; he was 8 then, but I don't remember… I don't remember much of anything before that. He took me into the bedroom where I thought my two sisters were. Snaper was 2 and Ember just a baby, but I hadn't seen her before and wondered when mama had delivered her. I had heard her cry, but had never seen her. I didn't know how babies were born, but I'd heard people talk about delivering them. I closed my eyes tight. I had a habit of doing that when I was scared."

"You can open your eyes now." River said.

The two little ones were gone. *"Where are my sisters? They were just here. I heard them."*

"I put them in mama's room." He said putting his arms around me. *"You need to rest. I want you to sleep and forget all about this."*

"What was daddy doing? Why was he hurting her? She didn't like it."

"You just pretend you didn't see it and it will all go away."

"Why did they call you River?" When I was upset, I tended to jump from one thought to another; to escape I guess… maybe"

"They didn't want me, so they didn't name me until I was born; then I just got named after the town… River's Bend."

"I just learned the name of our town this morning." I said. *"From the mailman."*

"I know. Now go to sleep."

"Don't go."

"I'll be here when you need me." Then he tucked me in bed and left.

When Echo's secretary had stuck her head in to announce her next patient, she had raised her hand and signaled her away.

Now Rain had become silent, her breathing even and slightly shallow; she was asleep. For the first time in her career, Echo did not know if she should wake her patient. She let her sleep and with appologies, asked her next patient to return at the end of the day and she would stay and see him then.

If Rain didn't wake before the following patient was due, then she would have to wake her and that would be fine by then… she was sure.

Chapter 2

BREEZE SAT QUIETLY AT THE end of the bar, where her view of the bar and all who entered was complete. Last week she had been Cinderella, and her Prince had very little imagination as he took her in that not so elegant horse drawn carriage.

Tonight she was Maid Marian. She was hoping to find a Robin Hood and the God of Wine and Passion to compete for her favors or even better… compete in giving her favors.

She dressed the part well and that always increased the number of suitors for her to choose from. She was a picky bitch and had a very select process of elimination. First she looked into their eyes… a deep sadness worked, but she preferred a twinkle, a spark or eyes that flashed with life. If the eyes revealed none of these they were unacceptable. Next she awaited the smile. Did it tease, did it tempt, was there power in it or was it a quivering shy attempt to please. Any of these would pass the test, all others would fail regardless of the eyes.

The third and final test of elimination was the dance. A man without rhythm would not perform well in bed. She wasn't looking for a relationship, she did not want a boyfriend… she wanted the "Fairy Tale". Since she was well aware that "Happily Ever After" did not exist, no one man could fill the part she required more than once or twice. After that she was bored and he was eliminated and she would shop again.

She was rarely wrong in her choice as she had been last week. It had only happened once before and she would be more aware from now on. She added to her list of eliminations; she would test the kiss and be more aware of how his fingers graced her skin. Her finesse in the art of the physical was learned early and her only teacher was what each touch made her feel… good, bad or indifferent.

It was 10:30 and the hunt stopped here. She usually needed to chose by 11:30 in order to have a full night to play out her "Fairy Tale", but tonight was different. Tonight she would eliminate either Robin Hood or the God of Wine and Passion. The rest of this fantacy would be played out in the woods… in the light of day.

Tonight she started with seven suitors; all had passed the eye test and the smile. As they guided her around the dance floor, three fell by the wayside. Then, one followed her out for a line dance and he was every bit her equal. He was a shoo-in and when the music stopped, he grabbed her and kissed her with such perfection that she was ready to lead him right out the door and forget the rest of her plan; she did not.

Three men remained from which to chose her 2nd choice, but first she made her claim on Jessie… explaining her plan. She found his intrigue and willingness to play, in perfect pitch with each test he'd passed. As remaining contestent number one led her to the dance floor, she felt the sweat of his hands and slipped from his grip. When she looked closer, his forehead was also covered in sweat and the back of his shirt and under his arms… how could she have missed that. Before he could reclaim her hand she excused herself to the bathroom.

Upon her return she simply stepped up to the bar, pressed her body up against contestant number two and kissed him with entheusium that was returned in a sloppy, submissive, irritating way. *'Another one bites the dust.' She thought.* Maybe she should have taken Jessie and ran like she'd been tempted to do. She hadn't, and now it was too late. She waited for contestant number three to saunter over, as she knew he would.

He did. His finger glided gently down her arm. With his other hand just below her waist, he pulled her to him, so that she would feel the firmness of his desire for her. The hand moved from her arm to her chin and turning her face up to him he kissed her. It was slow and gentle at first, but when he felt the tingle move to her nipples, making them hard against his chest, the kiss became inflamed. *'Thank god I waited for Jessie's competition.' She thought.*

Jack was not so inclined to play the game and compete; he wanted all of her, but because he wanted her badly enough, in the end he'd agreed. She knew now though, that she wanted them both right to the end of the "Fairy Tale". The competition tonight would be to see who played which part.

"You are an evil selfish bitch." She thought, as a physical shudder of excitement vibrated through her. With a smile she led them both to her truck and took them home; not her home of course… the hotel she had set up, that they were eager to pay for.

******

Music in the background, lights low, they stood at the bedside… there were no awkward moments. Jessie was kissing her with the simpleness of the early stages of desire. Jack was behind her caressing her derriere'. This was her first experience with more than one partner. As she began slowly to undress Jessie, Jack began to undress her in like manor. Someone was kissing or caressing someone as each inch of skin was uncovered.

When Jessie and Breeze stood naked, she turned to Jack and began the trail of nibbling from his shoulders to his toes, as his clothes began to fall to the floor. While she was busy at her task, Jessie's fingers tweaked and played with her nipples. As she moved lower on Jack, Jessie moved lower on her and his fingers tangled in her curls; one hand seeking access to the little nodule hidden there, while the other slipped two fingers into the warm wet cave from the back. She sucked in a deep breath and whimpered out a little moan.

"My god Maid Marian," Jessie whispered. "…Not only wet, but the heat of red hot coals."

She pushed against his fingers as she moved down and took Jacks bulging member between her lips. His gasp was like a match to gasoline, as the blistering heat ignited and the waves of pleasures began. Jessie's finger slid from her and his eager manhood moved inside her.

It wasn't long before the uncontrolled frenzy turned imputant, as the awkward positioning backfired and they all tumbled to the floor in a pile of laughter.

"Somehow my fantacy did not include seeing the "God of Wine and Passion" and Robin disassembling into a pile of giggling." She sputtered.

Jack and Jessie looked at each other with a grin and shaking their heads said, "Neither did mine."

The sizzling frenzy had passed and the awkwardness of trying to rekindle it was exasperating. This was to have been her first three-some and now it was a nothing. The easy moment was gone and sadly, Maid Marian was blushing?!?!

"Not possible." She thought, but she could feel the heat in her face as she covered herself with the sheet.

"I'm sorry." Jessie said, "are you alright?"

Jack answered for her. "She' not only fine; she runs on hot… that fire will burst into flames again in no time. Care to wager?"

She didn't like his words. This wasn't her… Breeze was a quiet, mind your own business, plain Jane. This wasn't real; this was her "Fairy Tale" and she should not be made to feel sleezy for it.

Jessie glared at him and pulled her into his arms. "What say we get a little sleep and pick this up later… in the morning as planned."

"Yes, thank you." She said, snuggling into his arms.

"Can't wait." Jack responded, hunkering down and resting one hand on her breast.

As she drifted off, she thought, *"At the bar Jack was in the lead for the God of Wine and Passion, but his class for the part has slipped away."* When she woke, a couple of hours later, Jessie was watching her and she could feel him absorbing her, as if he was drawing Breeze out of the Maid. It scared her; if he saw the real her… he'd run. But he locked his eyes to hers, slipped a finger under her chin and lifted her face to him, kissing her… not with passion, not with a decision to comply with his agreement. This kiss was tender and gentle, respectfully treating her as precious and breakable; yet firm enough to let her know he wanted her.

"He must not have seen the me inside after all… he still sees Maid Marian, but as a Queen." She thought.

Slowly with light caresses, intoxicating kisses and firm touches in secret places, the gentleness turned into fire burning passion. They didn't intend to include or even wake Jack; this was special… between them. He moved her slowly on top of him, lifting her over his ample appendage and lowering her, she muffled her squeel of pleasure with her hand as he entered.

They were unaware that Jack was already awake… watching as his cock grew and he became hard as flint. He would wait until they finished and then take his turn.

The ride was slow with an easy rhythm at first, but the rising of sensations were powerful… mind altering and the sounds of pleasure and need were less controlled.

"Not yet." He whispered. "Slow down." He pulled her down to him, taking a breast between his lips and suckeled as jolts of pleasure shot to every nerve in her body and she came spasming around him.

"Oh woman, stop; I don't want to cum yet."

At that Jack could stand it no more. He was watching her cum all over Jessie's cock inside her. She was leaned over with her ass in the air and he had to have her now. In one swift move he was behind her and pushing into her derriere'. She screamed in pain; he stopped, letting his erection rest in her. She was panting now, trying to adapt to the pain so she could speak.

"I'm sorry." Jack said. "Have you not done that before?"

"No… no, god it hurts."

"Relax, I won't move. I'll let you get used to it. We'll go slow, but you two got me so hot I just…"

"Do you want him off?" Jessie asked.

"I don't want him to move, not yet… it hurts."

Jessie took her face in his hands and kissed her with unexpected passion. He began to move again as his shrinking erection began to grow. When she began to move with him she felt the appendage behind her slide slowly back and forth as she and Jessie moved together. Jack didn't seem to be moving at all; just letting them massage his cock for him. Little by little the pain subsided, but she could not describe the feeling that replaced it. There was still pain, but not as extreem, it didn't feel good, but it didn't feel bad. She was terrified of Jack moving at all.

Jessie's throaty outbursts revealed his need to cum, her own cry of readiness set off a chain reaction… she came and Jack began to add nasty, dirty words, indicating his nearness of climax. Jessie came with hard final thrusts as Jack began to move into his own strides. She heard these words as though they belonged to someone else… "Stop…".

Jack emptied himself in her; she screamed again in pain as he pulled out and collapsed on the bed next to her.

They lay in silence, catching their breath; thinking.

"You liked that?" Jack asked.

"No, there was too much pain and why would you do that without asking me?" Her voice was shaky, angry… hostile. She had climaxed, but it wasn't good, not satisfying or pleasant at all. This was never going to happen again.

"Sorry Maid Marian; I thought you'd like it and you guys got me so hot, what else could I do?"

"Leave." She whispered, without hope of it happening.

"Leave? What about tomorrow?"

"I'll give up tomorrow before I take you. Please just go."

"My cars at the bar."

"Take a cab." Jessie said firmly.

"Okay, you and Robin Hood have a nice day tomorrow."

No one spoke while he dressed and left. No one spoke while Jessie held her as she fell asleep. No one spoke of what had just happened ever again.

Chapter 3

In the morning she got her bag and began to dress... in her regular clothes.

"Hey, what are you doing?"

"Getting Dressed."

"What about our plans? Those aren't Maid Marian clothes."

"But…"

"No buts… You are Maid Marian, I am Robin Hood and my title is… the God of Wine and Passion."

"You'd do that for me?"

"That's why I'm here pretty lady."

She hit the bathroom, showered and dressed… once again she was Maid Marian and filled with confidence; eager to see what the day would bring.

Robin Hood emerged from the bathroom and in his red satchal he carried the bottle of wine with the two wine glasses. On his head, around his hat, he wore the ring of leaves that was the crown of the God of Wine and Passion. In his hand he held the sceptre.

She wanted to giggle with glee, but she had to maintain the lady-like, proper role she had chosen.

****

He'd held her hand all the way up the mountain. When she parked, he flew around the truck to take her hand and help her down. He handed her the blanket and picnic basket, grabbed his satchal and sceptre and they headed out in different directions, as she instructed.

It was a warm day; perfect for a walk in the woods... she spread out her blanket, set the basket on the edge of it and removed her peti-coat for comfort. Laying down on her stomach, she grabbed her book and began to read. As she lay quietly under that Aspen, she began to feel warm. The sun only peeked through the trees and there was just the slightest of breeze; none the less, she hiked her skirt up to her bottom, just covering the butt cheeks.

****

In another part of the woods was Robin Hood. She had not told him where she would be or how to find her. She'd sent him off in another direction, with instructions to walk for 10 minutes before turning to look for her. He had no idea which way she went, but he was intrigued and determined to play the game just as she requested.

He had hoped for perfume, but she hadn't worn any. He recalled last night, how she smelled at the height of her arousal and even now it made his manhood twitch; he was entranced with the need of her. He continued trekking through the woods, looking, listening, smelling like a wolf eager to find his prey.

****

Still feeling warm, she unbuttoned her blouse to feel the breeze on her bossom; as an after thought, she moved off the blanket to the cool grass, raised the front of her skirt as well and returned to her previous position; feeling the cool grass on her skin she began once again to read.

****

15

After a sharp turn in direction, his stare was fixed on the erotic sight before him. As she lay on the grass, her feet crossed in the air with her knees slightly parted... he wondered if she was aware that she was revealing the treasure between her thighs to him.

"Do you know I am here?" he wondered. She knew he'd be coming, but she didn't know how long it would take him to find her or from which direction he was coming... unless she heard him. *"Was she the wolf instead of him?"* He wondered. He sat down in the grass to watch her... his mouth watered as his eyes moved up and down her body and back to the silent revelation between her thighs.

Pausing for a moment she peered over the top of her book, looking around as though she'd heard something; pretending not to know he was there. He was sitting not more than 10 feet away.

She looks at him, pretending not to see him. She is trying to read his face; his reaction to the temptation she so carefully placed before him... being as coy as she knew how to be. She shuddered, a little surprised at how arousd she was at the site of his eyes so mesmerizingly fixed on her crotch.

She stretches with a little moan as she allows her legs to open a little further. She turns back to her book, but she senses him slithering a little closer; her heart racing in anticipation. A twig cracks under his foot and he stops less than 3 feet away to await her reaction.

"What if he wants to eat first... we didn't have breakfast and it's nearly 1:00." She thought with disappointment sneaking in, but the tingle in her belly told her that was not likely.

She waits and then releases just the slightest of a whimpering sigh. Now he's sure that she knows he's there, and moving to his hands and knees he crawls over until... still on his hands and knees, he is hovering over her body. His hand gently rests on her leg behind her knee and she can feel his warm breath. The aroma, with which his body is pleading, fills her nostrils and makes her nipples hard.

His hand glides up the outside of her thigh, slowly circling and moving, until he discovers the very treasure his eyes had beheld. She can feel the smile move across his face, just as she feels the smile move across hers.

She felt him pushing against her, and now knowing for sure that he was hard caused a spasm of need letting him know that she was ready too. She bit her bottom lip as she turned to look at him.

"Don't do that; it makes me jealous."

"Jealous?? Of what?"

"Jealous of **your** teeth biting that lower lip. I want to do that myself."

He rolled her on to her back and on to the blanket. Now her pussy was in full view. His eyes drank it all in, the lips around it swollen, her tiny nodule swollen and ready. He knelt between her legs and breathed in the now familiar aroma. He leaned down and ran his tongue along her inner thigh. She gasped softly as his warm tongue touched her skin.

Inch by inch, she gasps again as his tongue moves onto her wet lips; she closes her eyes as he parts those lips with his fingers and begins running his tongue up and down her wet slit, tasting her.

She feels his tongue slide over the entrance and she moans slightly. He works his tongue deep inside, poking and probing as her heart beats faster. His tongue feels like a small cock as it probes to please her; taking her to the edge. He eases his fingers inside her, exploring her depths as he takes her clit into his mouth. He licks, he sucks, he licks, he sucks… driving her mad with need; the tension building, building while his fingers continued their work inside her. She grabs his head and pushes hard against his face; he sucks harder, circling with his tongue. At last her body begins to shudder, her legs start to quake and the tension stiffens her body just before the orgasm releases her. He didn't think she could be any wetter … he was wrong.

As the orgasm begins to subside, she lifts his head and pulls him up to her, kissing the juices from his face; tasting her satisfaction on his tongue.

His crown had fallen off and now he placed it on her head. He stood and took a step back. She was smiling to herself, thinking of the effect she was having on him. His straining manhood was now begging for some sort of release of its own. All the sexual tension that had welled up inside of him while looking at her, smelling her and touching her, was now in a heightened state. She saw his hand moving as he started rubbing his crotch. She gasped with pleasure at seeing the huge bulge. She continued to watch as his hand began groping, gripping and rubbing his cock through his trousers. She felt herself getting wetter; her nipples ached even more than before.

She opened her blouse to expose her breasts and to let him see just how hard her nipples had become; just from watching him tease his cock through his trousers. She wanted to watch the cum spurting from him and raining down onto her breast, coating them with his semen, but even more she wanted him inside her. He unzipped his Robin Hood trousers, slipped his hand inside and set his manhood free. His hand moved slowly up and down his throbbing cock, but his eyes are fixed on hers. She's staring at him, anticipating the pleasure he's going to give her... running her tongue over her lips eager for the taste of him.

Then his fingers close around his cock, now rockhard. She looked up into his eyes. Both he and his firm appendage appeared to be begging her to take over the stroking and begin the sucking that would bring him to a much needed release.

Until this very moment, neither of them had spoken a word and she wondered if they ever would. He took a step forward as she sat upright; she grabbed his pants and pulled them down to his knees. As he lifted each foot she removed them.

Slipping her fingers around its ample girth she sucked him in between her lips; first toying with the tip and then sucking him in as deep as she could. She began stroking him with her lips over and over again. His throaty groans assured her his pleasure was enhanced by her touch. She replaced her lips with her fingers as she moved back and took the softer toys into her mouth, playing with them gently. She carried him right to the edge and stopped.

"You, my sweet Maid Marion, are amazing." He panted, reaching down and pulling her to her feet... embracing her and kissing her, with the same glass like respect and gentle caring that he had in his kiss the night before. Then very slowly he removed every stitch of clothing she was wearing. While she watched he finished undressing himself. They sat down together, quite Adam and Eve. He pulled the wine and glasses from his satchel and poured them each a glass.

She didn't want wine... she wanted him, but the God of Wine and Passion had mesmerized her, and she could only follow his lead.

"To Fairy Tales and Maid Marian and to the woman within." He said, lifting his glass. "I am ever grateful to have found you."

"To you, my God of Passion... To you, Robin Hood, the soul mate of Maid Marian, To you, the greatest hero of all my Fairy Tales."

They drank and he gently lay her back, kissing her forehead, temples, nose, chin... She trembled as desire moved through her. He kissed her shoulder, poured wine on her breasts and devoured them... a jolt of passion consumed her. He filled her naval and drank from it... heat flowed between her thighs. His kisses truned to nibbles when they reached her toes and he nibbled his way back up. When he reached her lips, his tongue slipped between them, searching for her tongue... sucking it into his mouth. His knee moved between her legs and she opened for him. He slipped easily inside her as a sigh of pleasure escaped her lips.

The sensations of pleasure escalated higher and higher; she had never felt this high before... *"this man of magic had surpassed her wildest dream. This was just sex, but it didn't feel like just sex... but we've only just met; it could be nothing more."* Her thoughts vanished as he carried her into an orgasm that left her weak and trembling. In his arms with her head on his chest... he too was still trembling.

****

Her head was spinning on the drive back to town. He was talking about all sorts of nothing and though she heard him, she had no idea what he'd said. Her own thoughts had consumed her. *"I can't see him again; not even 2 or 3 times... not at all. I could love this one and that would only mean heart break. No man can love a girl like me. Anyway, if by some miracle he did... he'd find out the real me; the nobody. He'd run like hell and that would hurt even worse."*

When he asked for her number she took his. When he asked her name she replied... Maid Marian. When he asked when he could see her again she said, "I don't know. My schedule is tight, but I have your number."

"I want to see you again… soon." He said. "You're a little crazy, but I love it."

"But would you love it after a year?"

"After a lifetime I think." He responded with a grin.

"Then you're thinking with your little boy toy there."

"That too, but there is something about you. I just can't…"

"Put your finger on it?"

He pulled her to him and kissed her and though it was quite convincing as to his sincerity, she was sure it was a warning of disaster. Still, she was unable to not respond to his kiss.

She got back in her truck and he closed the door. As he got in his truck he called out, "Maid Marian, call me. If you don't, I will find you and I will live out my life as Robin Hood if I have to." Then he winked at her and tipped his hat. He was still dressed as Robin Hood, but when he got in his truck, he traded that hat for a cowboy hat.

"Hummm, he wasn't wearing a hat when she met him… was he wearing cowboy boots?" She pondered.

Chapter 4

"BOY HOWDY LITTLE LADY."

Ember looked up at the biggest, brightest smile she'd ever seen, as the man before her clicked the heels of his cowboy boots together, tipped his hat and said, "Ma'am."

The words, "Can I help you?" fell from her mouth, but the smile on her face was quite frozen and she wasn't sure she could ever move her lips to speak again.

"Why yes ma'am; I think you can. How 'bout a real tall cup of the blackest coffee you got and if you could recommend a good breakfast cake, tha'd be fine."

She stood there unable to move, speak or even breathe.

"Ember!!"

Her head jerked around to look behind her so fast she was sure she got whiplash. If she didn't feel it now, she would by tomorrow.

The kid behind her jerked his head nodding toward the customer. It worked; she turned back to him with, "Yes sir, I'll get that for you right away."

She pulled out her favorite coffee cake and her friend handed her his coffee.

"Here you are sir. Sorry about the wait."

He just grinned at her; clearly amused by her nervousness.

"If you'll take that over to the casheer she'll get you checked out right away."

"Thank you pretty lady… and the wait was a pleasure."

He winked and moved along, but the next day he was back… in her line. And the next day. She felt like a giggly school girl and it made her self-consious.

She only worked there 3 days a week and wondered if he'd ever be back, but she was quite a 'what will be will be' kinda girl. She was sure, if she pushed anything into happening it would explode in her face. *"He's just flirting; it doesn't mean anything. I'm sure he does it everywhere he goes.'* She thought to herself.

****

When she got back to work there was an envelope with her name on it. Her co-workers were staring in anticipation.

"Where did this come from; it's not a pink slip is it? I need this job."

"Ember just open it; we want to know."

It was a simple, but elegant thank you card and the note read…

> Thank you Bright Eyes, for taking your time with me and sharing your warm smiles. I send my voice dancing in the wind with it's warm and gentle caress. And in my mind's eye, I see the laughter in your eyes and I wait to see you again to find that your words gently fall off your soft lips to enter my soul.
>
> Every Sincerely,
> Task

She looked up at her co-workers. "Who left this?"

They all nodded toward the counter and as she turned to look, the cowboy stood before her grinning.

She could feel her body tremble, but she stood tall, shoulders back and with a big smile she stepped up to the counter.

"Did you leave this for me?" she asked, holding the card out to him.

"Good morning Bright Eyes; I did. If I was too presumptuous, I apologize, but it was an impulse and I was obligated to follow it. If I come in later, will you have coffee with me… or tea or milk or what ever your heart desires?"

"Wow, that's a mouthful for a man."

"I love the way your eyes laugh."

"Tell the man to come back and have coffee with you lady; I'm in a hurry. Hit on her on your own time buddy."

"I'm sorry." He stepped aside and waited patiently while she waited on the next 10 customers.

He ordered coffee only and repeated his question. "If I come back will you have some sort of drink with me?"

"Four o'clock. There's a pub 4 doors down; I'll have a Colorado Bulldog."

****

She walked in and waited for her eyes to adjust. She looked around… twice; he wasn't there.

Disappointed, far more than she thought she should be, she was about to turn around and leave when the bartender called out, "Bright Eyes; that's you, right? You looking for a Colorado Bulldog?"

Surprised and confused she walked up to the bar. "How did you…?"

"This guy came in this morning, said he was to meet a lady at 4:00, but was working and might not make it on time. He gave me $50 and said to keep you in whatever you wanted and to offer you a menu. Then he handed me a $20 tip and said to tell you he was sorry and he'd be here the moment he got off work… please wait."

"Serious?"

"Damn straight."

She sat down and took a sip of her drink. She refused the menu and went to play the juke box. At 4:40 he slid on to the stool next to her. "I am so sorry Bright Eyes, but I was afraid if I told you I might not get off work in time, you might back out. I'm so glad you waited; thank you."

"You managed to make getting stood up intriguing, but I wouldn't recommend attempting a re-run."

He threw his head back in a big ole Texas laugh... at least that's the only way I can think of describing it. Being the mouse in the corner... observing, I have a limited vocabulary. When the Crow on the highline pole is the observer, you might find it more flowery.

"No re-runs for the lady. Straight up from now on."

"Are you a real cowboy or do you just dress the part?"

"Don't live on a ranch, but my grandfather did. I've ridden a horse a time or two, but I couldn't rodeo. I exaggerate the cowboy thing when I'm trying to impress a lady, but it feels comfortable to me. I like getting out by myself and sleeping on the ground when life gets heavy. I've milked a cow, driven a tractor and once I helped my grandfather herd the cattle. I can do a pretty good two-step and I love to look at the sky, day or night. You tell me, am I a cowboy?"

"I guess I don't know. I've never met a real cowboy, so I have nothing to compare to."

"My family history is real cowboys and I feel kind of like I'm a real cowboy, but I'm just a man. Just a man that would rather be talking about you. What's your real name Bright Eyes?"

"Ember."

"Aaww yes... Beautiful. I remember hearing it now at the coffee shop."

"Why... how is that beautiful?"

"If I close my eyes, I see a blazing fire in all it's glory warming the world and as it burns down slowly the red hot ember, however small, remains equally as beautiful. With my eyes open I see that red glowing ember that never dies, but is constant in it's warmth and beauty. I see you."

"Oh my god; you do have a silver tongue. Should I be wary?"

"The words may be silver, but they hold the power of truth as strong as pure gold. You should always be wary, but be careful not to confuse being cautious with fear. Caution will protect you; fear will either steal what wonder life has for you or destroy you; don't partake of it."

"Ohhh, you really have to stop that."

"Okay... moving on. Family? Brothers, sisters?"

"No, no one."

"Only child?" he asked.

"No, they're just gone. It was a long time ago. I'd rather not..." *Meeting my family would put an end to his interest instantly.'* She thought.

"I'm sorry. What should we..."

"Your grandfather... the cowboy; talk about him."

"Your kidding; you don't really want to hear my grandfather stories?"

"Yes I do."

"Okay, you asked for it. There was this one time when there was a new archaeological discovery near an old stage coach depot. My grandpa and I hopped on our motorcycles and headed up there. He was buff at that sort of thing and I loved doing it with him. They'd found the remains of a horse and rider and when we got there my gramps friend, who was one of the archeologists, lifted up the saddle bag and handed it to my gramps. The paper was old, but the letters were still in tact. We went inside the tent to use special tools to remove the letters in hopes of keeping them in tact, and maybe even getting them to the relatives of the recipients at some point. That's where I could help; finding people and / or their relatives is something I'm good at."

"And did you?"

"There were 6 letters. Two fell apart; too crumbled to decifer, but the others were still readable. The family line ended with the recipient in 1 of them. There was no finding one of them at all. The other two eventually got to great, great, great grands or whatever."

"That's amazing."

"I thought so. Dance with me."

He did indeed do a fine two-step and a little more.

The music slowed and the song was unfamiliar, but too slow even for a two-step so he held her, swaying gently. When the song ended he didn't release her and she looked up at him. His kiss was gentle, his tongue warm and sweet as it circled hers. It was as though it belonged there.

Chapter 5

RAIN SETTLED IN ON THE couch as Echo crossed her legs and prepared to take notes. Their second session was about to begin.

"I'd like to begin today with you telling me more about your family; your sisters. To make it simple, let's go from the oldest to the youngest. Is that acceptable to you?"

"You're the doctor. I want to do whatever you feel is best. That's fine… so I guess I'll start with Snaper." Hearing the name from her lips shocked her. She had rarely said it before and now that she was dead, she hadn't spoken it at all. It was like she never existed unless, like now, someone asked about her.

"Good then, tell me about Snaper."

"She was 2 years younger than me and the only thing I remember about her, before she was 13, was that sometimes in the night when I was sad, alone… scared, she would come in and crawl into my bed and put her arm around me. She never spoke and when I woke up she was gone."

"You said she **was** 2 years younger than you; what did you mean?"

"Snaper was the sister who died a year ago."

"I'm sorry; would you rather begin with someone else?"

"It doesn't matter. It won't change anything, unless of course you think it would be better."

"Let's go on with her then, but if it gets too difficult we'll stop."

"Okay. She was very beautiful, but always angry. I think she hated everyone. At first I thought it was puberty cause it started when she was 13. She wasn't around much, but when I saw her she was always angry."

"Did you ever figure out why; was it just puberty?"

"No, but I didn't get it. It was River who told me what happened that made her so mad. My sisters, we didn't see much of each other; we were all so different. I rarely saw any of my sisters, but for some reason, River always knew what was going on with them. They all told him everything and I think he unburdened himself a little by telling me. Kind of like I need you to talk to... he needed me."

"That makes sense. Your brother must love and trust you very much to take you into his confidence that way."

"I guess so. Like I said, he's the only one that I know that ever really loved me. He told me once, *"You're special and I don't want you to have sex; I want you to stay clean and pure until you're deeply in love... until you are fully secure in that love. Then it will be beautiful; not ugly. But I want you to learn about it; how it is with and without love. I will help you learn from your sister's experiences... the good and the bad."* I didn't understand; I still don't understand, but I think it's for my own good."

"Has he ever approached you sexually? Has he..."

"Oh god no!! He's my brother. Why would you ask that?"

"To hear your answer."

"My answer is no."

She wasn't sure why, but Echo believed her. "Good. Go on then."

"About River or Snaper?"

"Your sister."

"Like I said, she was beautiful and all the guys wanted to date her. She hung out with them, but never dated one on one. She could get them to do what ever she wanted. She got one of them to give her his motorcycle for her 14th birthday. River said she rode the bike all the time. She bought biker clothes and skipped school looking to get into a biker club, but River said, what she found in stead was more like a biker gang."

****

"Hey kid, what the hell you doing way out here all alone?"

"I want to join your club."

"Club? You do huh? This ain't no fucking club little pussy. This is a gang, and if you still want to hook up with us, you'll need to see our lead. Want a beer?"

"Tha'd be great; I'd love one." She was smoking; had been for 2 years already, but she'd never had alcohol before. That's what River said."

She went on… "They played around with her for a while, feeding her beer after beer till she was tipsy. They kept the other girls away from her; no contact allowed until and unless she was ushered into the gang or club. They'd kiss her, cop a little titty feel and tease her. Then they took her in the back room to Jasper. He kicked them all out except his top three men.

"What's this?" He asked, nodding to the girl.

"She rode in here on her bike and said she wanted to join with us."

"That so?" He asked, looking right at her.

"Yes."

"Were you sober when you got here; you're not now."

"Yes I was; Jasper is it?"

"You want to call me by my first name little pussy? Only if you're calling it out when I fuck you."

She could feel her eyes getting big and she forced control. These pricks would not get the best of her, but pricks or not, she wanted to be a member of their club. She was tired of looking and now that she found one, it was time to join.

"When the time is right then… sir." She replied.

She wasn't sure how to feel about the roar of laughter that came from these four men. *"Skanky men."* She thought, but she'd looked around and they weren't all skanky. *"That tall one could use a bath though."* She felt her nose crinkle.

"You sure you want to join us?" Jasper asked.

"Quite sure."

"What do you boys say? Should we take this little pussy in?"

They were all enthusiastically affirmative.

"What's your name?"

"Snaper."

"Real name."

"Snaper."

"For real bitch?"

"Yes."

"You know there's initiation?"

"In all clubs I would expect that."

"You realize all four of us are going to fuck you."

Her breath caught in her throat. She forced herself to suck air into her lungs and then more or less gasped out, "When the time is right then sir."

"The time is right now."

She could no longer hide her panic. Her voice shaking as she said, "Ma-maybe I sh-should co-co-come back in a few d-days."

"It's too late for that now. You made your decision. Let the initiation begin."

They moved toward her, she ran for the door, but it was pointless. They held her arms; the desk behind which Jasper had sat was now cleared and he was taking off his belt as they lay her on it in front of him. One held her arms and the other two each took a leg removing her boots and then her jeans.

She lay before him naked from the waist down. He ripped her blouse open and when he saw those pert young titties, without the need of a bra, he devoured them; sucking hard as she cried in pain.

"Hold her head, so she can watch my cock fill her up." Jasper rasped in his husky voice of sexual need. He spread her lips and pounded his hard cock on her clit. She squirmed and wiggled to get free, but it was useless.

He laid it at the entrance of her opening and pushed, she was tight; he thrust again filling her as she screamed. His head was thrown back as he felt the tightness of her caressing his cock as he thrust. His mouth open, his grunts of escalating pleasure; he couldn't last long with a pussy this tight. He wanted to watch his cock fill her, but when he looked down he stopped.

"What the fuck is this? There's blood everywhere. Are you a fucking virgin?"

She could only nod.

"What the hell; how old are you?"

"14."

"14!?!?!? What the fuck have you guys gotten us into?" But the words "virgin pussy" were screaming in his head and in the blink of an eye, shock and fear were replaced with a craving for it; a lust that was unsurpassed. He lost all control, watching as he took ownership of her bloody pussy... grunting and cussing, he rammed her until the screaming stopped and she fell silent. He looked to see that she hadn't passed out and she turned her face away. He came spurting semen in her, on her... He knew he would take her again and again before this day was done, but now he had to honor the initiation. He stepped aside.

Toro moved up to the desk; his 7-inch cock hard in his hand. He leanded over and kissed her and she threw up. He'd pulled away just in time and someone wiped the puke away.

"Bitch!!" he yelled as he grabbed her and flipped her to her stomach. He spread her and entered, leaned over and grabbed each breast pulling her against him and began the deep hard thrusts.

There was pain and she whimpered continuely, but before long the sensation of pain was overwhelmed by another sensation that she did not recognize. It became stronger and stronger, her insides tightened around his huge cock and she was no longer whimpering, she was cuming, again and again.

Toro pulled out and wiped his bloody cock on her shirt. Willy moved toward the desk, but Jasper stopped him.

"Hold on a minute. The kid was a virgin… she's gotta hurt. Send in one of the girls to clean her up and feed her if she wants food. We'll come back later and take up where we left off."

"What the fuck am I supposed to do with this?" Willy asked shaking his stiff dick at Jasper.

"If I were you, I'd go wash it; it smells nasty… just use cold water. When was your last shower anyway?"

"Fuck you ass hole; it's only been a week."

"Jesus Christ Willy; go take a shower."

One of the girls came in and they left her to do her work. She washed Snaper as she lay unmoving, still on the desk. She made her get up and finish herself. Snaper refused food, but drank 3 bottles of water one after the other. She wanted to dress, but was not allowed.

The girl never spoke to her other than to tell her to get up and finish cleaning herself and offering her food.

She lay on the couch and was covered with a blanket. She had almost fallen asleep when the four men came back in. Willy hadn't bothered to dress after his shower and was only wearing a towel which he dropped immediately as he pulled the blanket off of her. He knelt between her legs on the couch and grabbing her knees, pulled her butt on to his lap and shoved all 4 inches inside her. He pounded till he was done and walked away. "Antonio, the pussy is all yours; nothing special just tighter than most."

"Has to be," Tony said, "for that little cock of yours to get off."

Fists were up and ready, but Jasper told Willy to get the hell out and get dressed. "And don't put those stinky clothes back on. You got a woman; see to it she gets you some clean ones."

"Aawwhh, fuck you."

Tony moved to the couch and pulled Snaper to her feet. He wiped her gently with a wet cloth. He stood in front of her touching her gently… caressing. "I'm sorry they weren't gentle with you." He whispered softly. She whimpered.

He played gently with each nipple and then sat on the couch and probed the V with his tongue. "Open your legs." It was a demand, but not coarse… not abrasive. She obeyed, biting back another whimper.

His hand slid between her thighs and slipped inside her as his tongue probed the V again. He tried, but he wasn't very good at it and by now she was numb… drifting away fron this reality.

He lay her down and mounted her, but the look of misery on her face was shrinking his erection, so he lay behind her and pulled her back against him and raised her leg. He finished, kissed her cheek and thanked her… and then he was gone.

She picked the blanket off the floor and covered herself. Curling up in the fetal position, she hoped to sleep. That wasn't going to happen. Jasper was now ready to claim his prize and took her to his room. He had a woman too, but she knew better than to enter that room until she was invited; especially if there was a new initiation.

He took her over and over in every possible manor he could think of. Nothing he did could bring out any kind of response from her and soon he was tired of her.

Chapter 6

MORNING CAME AND HER FINAL initiation was today. She was unaware of it. She would pick three men from the club and naked on the bar, each would eat her until she screamed her orgasm for the whole club... men and women... to see. A contest of sorts.

Some of the men hated this because if it took a long time, it was a reflection on their manhood; yet thewatchers loved it... it made a great show. Any man without a woman of his own did not look forward to being chosen. Those with women however, were happy for the diversion and didn't care if it took all day. They could tell their woman to jerk them off while they did it if they wanted to.

Snaper was placed on the bar. She sat there, staring. Jasper had let her sleep most of the last 5 hours. She'd eaten and was instructed as to what she had to do. When it was over she would drink with the ladies until she passed out. The next morning she could go home to pack her things and would be expected to return to them by sunset. The honor system would prove her worth. She heard all this, but it was like she was a ghost in the corner and they were talking to someone else.

Last night she had thought, "*What have I gotten myself into? How had I let this happen. That motorcycle was supposed to bring fun and excitement into my life; that so far has not existed.*"

This morning she was angry, she was hurt, she felt dirty and used. She was afraid and her body was racked with pain, but now as she sat here naked on this bar, all she felt was overwhelmingly sad. The sadness was growing as her eyes became fixed. She stared, but saw nothing. She thought, but nothing in her mind made sense. She felt pain, but it didn't feel like it was in her body. She felt no urge to move.

It wasn't until she felt the sting of the hand on her face, not until she heard the cracking sound, like that of a breaking twig, that she realized someone had been talking to her. Her attention was required; that registered, but the focus to give them that attention evaded her.

Jasper raised his hand to hit her again. "Jasper wait!" Teanna, his woman, reached to stop his hand. "Look at her; she doesn't even know you are talking to her. I think she's in shock or something."

He stopped and looked at her. Her eyes still stared and the look on her face was so empty it scared him; though he'd never let that be known. "How do we snap her out of it?" He could not take his eyes off her. He'd never seen anything like it. Her face was even emptier than that of someone dead.

"I don't know, warmth maybe… and sleep I think might help."

"We don't have time for that coddling. We move out day after tomorrow. She has to be back and ready to go. We have to get this finished."

"She can't choose in that condition. How will we choose?"

He stood quiet, watching her. *"Fuck!'* he thought. *"What the hell do I do? I have to take action fast."* He stood silent… then he turned. "She will chose by proxy."

They all looked at him like he was crazy. Half of them had no idea what 'proxy' was. Even if they had, Jasper has warped the true meaning.

"Teanna, 39 guys… get there names in a bowl or something. She can draw 3 names. When the eating starts she'll snap out of it."

******

He put the bowl in front of her face and said, "Snaper, pick from the bowl." She stared. He turned her face so she was looking at him, but he knew she didn't see him. "Snaper, god damn it, pick

34

from the fucking bowl." She stared. He picked up her hand and put it in the bowl. She didn't move it, but now she was staring at her hand.

"Get something sticky." He growled at Teanna.

"Why… what do you want?"

"You questioning me? Just get it!"

She returned with a squeeze bottle of honey.

"Hold the bowl."

She took it.

Jasper took Snaper's hand and squeezed honey on it, put it back in the bowl, moved it around and pulled it out. He held it up and yelled, "Proxy!" The place filled with cheers. *Not exactly proxy, but he wasn't aware of that.*

There were too many pieces of paper on her hand. He shook it and one by one they fell off until only 3 remained. He called them out. "Ben." Ben was 52, had been with them since he was 19. He had been lead, but turned it over to Jasper when he had his heart attack, 4 years ago. The condition had been that Jasper's spot be filled by Willy, his son, when the time came. It was the only chance the dim wit would have.

"Roy." Roy was 22, had been with them 2 years and at 6'3", made of pure muscle… no one gave him any shit.

"Sockher." His name was Chad, but he aquired the nick-name his first year. Sockher was 39; had been with them 11 years. He was on his 3rd woman and he beat them all. It was frowned upon. It was okay to smack em around a little, but fists were used on men; not women. The other men intervened if they were around. They warned him all the time and once they even broke his arm saying, 'a taste of his own medicine'. His first woman died with her baby in child birth. His second escaped 4 years ago after nearly dieing the 2nd time from a beating. They looked for her, but she had vanished well. Number 3 was tougher than he was, so she held her own and he liked it.

The men came forward and Snaper was laid back on the bar.

Ben sat on the bar stool between her legs and lifted them over his shoulder. The cheers were rising louder and louder. As he leaned in for his first taste, she whined a slight protest and squirmed as though somewhere, deep inside her, she remembered the feeling and didn't want it. Then her mind must have blocked it out because she lay there barely breathing and that was the only movement or sound that came from her body.

"Fuck Jasper, I can't do this. It's like eating the pussy of a dead woman. We either forfeit this part of the initiation or put it off till she snaps out of this."

"It's not the way…"

"Fuck the way; let's vote."

Jasper looked around; the cheers had subsided to nothing after the first 3 minutes. "Roy… Sockher… what do you want to do?"

"I say we just forget it." Roy shrugged.

"I get 5 minutes." Sockher insisted. "She's still dead in 5 minutes, nobody can wake her up."

Jasper put it up for a vote and they all agreed.

Ben moved out of the way and Sockher dove in for the kill; wasted time… his prey was already dead, so to speak.

****

Teanna wrapped a blanket around her and the girls helped her to bed. Order's were, if she woke up, she should be given alcohol and they should make her feel safe and comfortable. He wanted this zombie state to end. He didn't care what expression her face held, as long as it held one. He wished he could just take her home and leave her, but like it or not she was one of them now and he was responsible for her. If he left her behind, it would be considered abandonment and no one would trust him again.

Five hours passed before she moved. With the blanket tight around her she sat on the side of the bed looking around. She was trying to remember. They brought her clothes and took her to the bathroom to shower and dress. They brought her milk and green chili stew. As she finished it, they handed her a beer. She drank it; she remembered… nothing from that morning in the bar, but everything else was there; flooding back… overwhelming her mind. Teanna took one look at her and knew.

She put her arm around her. "It's okay. The initiation is over. They released you from this morning's games. Now you just get to know us. Then you're one of us."

"I don't want to be. I just want to go home."

"It's too late for that. You've been accepted. Jasper is responsible for you now. If he let you go home to stay, it would be seen as running out on you. They see that you came with a need to get away from home; we took you in. If you leave us without cause, they see him as abandoning you."

"But even if I want to go?"

"One woman, who was nearly beaten to death, escaped and it was allowed and not thought of as a black mark on Jasper. That is the only one."

"Do I have to..." she began to cry.

"To sleep with the guys? Not all the time. They get special treatment on birthdays and on some holidays they can pick a woman, but they have to treat her good; not get too rough. When a man wants you to be his woman, you have the choice, but if you chose him... he owns you."

"This is not what I thought it..." She fell silent.

"Tomorrow at sunrise you go home... you're on your honor to return. Don't make Jasper come after you. It won't be good for you if you do. You gather what you want... just what you can carry on your bike. You say good-bye to who you feel the need to and you come home to us. We are your home now; where ever we are... that's home."

"My family...?"

"They will be off limits from us, so no one will hurt them, but we are your family now." She handed her another beer.

****

"Snaper walked into the kitchen. Mom yelled at her for not coming home and made her eat. Then she went to her room and River was there waiting for her. He held her while she cried and then she must have told him everything." Rain fell silent.

37

"This was hear-say of course; from her brother, but what a traumatic thing to happen to a 14 year old. It didn't happen to Rain, but it was her sister and she had to have felt her pain." Echo's mind was spinning… sorting… wondering. They should be changing the line of thinking here, but it was not a good place to stop if Rain wanted to go on.

"Would you like to finish Snaper's story or pick it up another day?"

"I want to get it over with. I don't want to go back to it."

"Alright; go on then."

"River said she cried herself dry, talked like the dam busted and then disappeared into her body somewhere. He stayed with her all night. She got up the next morning and packed a bag and left without a word. He tried to follow her, but *'the damn traffic'* he said. He would look for her the next day… get an early start."

Chapter 7

"Snaper pulled off the road and drove back into the woods. She was supposed to have been there, to the club, by sunset yesterday. They'd be out looking for her soon, if they weren't already. She couldn't go back there and she couldn't go home. She had a full tank of gas in the bike and about $40. She sat in the leaves as the sun seeped through the trees warming her. Her mind was spinning; seeking an answer… where could she go?"

"She thought, she dozed… it was nearly 3:00 when she woke up. She had to do something. The bikers are north, home is south… she'd go east. She would just get on her bike and go east. She had her sleeping bag if she got tired. She'd packed enough food for at least three days; more if she was careful. She'd go until she'd used up 2 tanks of gas and see where it took her. Maybe she could stop there and find a way to… to what? She was 14, she couldn't get a job; if she went to a shelter they'd call the cops and send her home. If they sent her home the bikers would find her. There was no point in trying to figure it out now… she just had to go. She got on her bike and headed east."

****

"The next morning River went looking… Time passed and he never gave up. Then one day, she was there in my room, telling me she was tired of running and wanted to come home, but she didn't stay. When I told River he was furious; not that she didn't stay, but that she came back with nothing good to offer."

****

"Snaper pulled into the rest stop and parked in the back. She was badly in need of relief. She thought of stopping along the road, but it just didn't feel safe to her. She hadn't felt safe since she was 13.

"She felt better as she headed back to her bike; her face freshly washed and a moment of silence without thought had done wonders. As she stood there staring into the woods around the rest stop, she felt almost peaceful.

"*Maybe I should just stay here for the night. I have the woods to protect me, the bathroom close and I can wash up before I leave.*" She thought pondering. "*No, I should go farther away. I'm too close; they could find me.*"

"Indecision was something she was not used to feeling. She'd always known what she wanted and went for it… "*look where that got you, idiot.*" She yelled at herself in her head."

****

Rain fell silent and Echo waited. "I didn't sleep well that night. I tossed and turned and River and Snaper were zooming back and forth in my head; I was sure it meant she would be back or he'd find her, but…"

****

"It was 7:00 and another hour to the next town according to the road signs. She pushed the bike back into the woods. It would be dark soon. She pulled out the bag with food and ate skimpily. She leaned back against the tree and closed her eyes listening to the sounds of the earth, the birds… she let them take her away.

"A twig snapped and she sat up straight. She opened her eyes, looking around. Dusk had set in and she couldn't see well, but after 5 minutes of semi-panic, she decided it was nothing. She pulled out her sleeping bag, removed her shoes, pants and shirt and crawled in, using her clothes as a pillow.

"Hours passed; something woke her and the panic building within her made no logical sense. No one was at the rest stop when she went into the woods, wild animals did not frighten her... there was no reason to think she was not safe and yet fear gripped at her. Her stomach twisted, her heart was pounding.

"She opened her eyes. There was no moon and the stars gave nearly no light. The light from the rest stop could barely be seen seeping through the trees. It was, at the very least, 50 yards away.

"Slowly she began to look around when her eyes froze on the silhouette; was it even a silhouette or just a tree, a shadow? She couldn't move, she was glued to this possible threat. *"What if it was just a shadow and the threat was coming from the other direction?"* Her mind was spinning, but her body and her eyes could not move.

"Her breathing was very deep, very slow and silent; maybe he wouldn't hear her... wouldn't see her. Her neck was beginning to hurt in this position and still she couldn't move. Fear held her tight.

"Then he was behind her, knelt down so she could smell him and he held a knife to her throat. The smell was familiar, but she was so frightened. She tried to think, but all the smells that bombarded her consciousness were the ones of the bikers... she threw up. Held tight with the knife it was all over her and his arm, but he never flinched.

"You ruined everything." he whispered; his voice raspy with emotion. "You have dirtied your life, you are not useful anymore and now you have no where to go. There is nothing you can do. These trees will not sustain you. I am sorry, but now you will rest."

"The pain lasted less than a split second, she felt the warm dampness as her blood flowed from her neck, she choked and it was over. He held her, he cried and he was gone."

****

Rain shuddered at the memory. "It may have been the moment she died that I woke up screaming. I wasn't close to her, but she had been in my head all night."

"How long was she gone before they found her?"

"I'm not sure. It was 4 days later when River called and told me. He said when they released the body he had her cremated and spread her ashes in the woods where she died."

"There was no funeral? Your parents, your sisters… no one got to say good-bye?"

"My parents didn't believe in funerals. He did the right thing."

"I know this has been stressful for you. We still have 30 minutes, but we can stop here if you'd like."

"I'm alright. I don't want to waste time; I want to fix me. I can't live like this."

"If you're sure then; which sister is next?"

"Ember, she's 30. She was just a baby the first time River helped me. At least the first time I remember."

"What would you like to tell me about Ember?"

"She works in a coffee shop part time. River said she met a cowboy recently and she's crazy about him, but she's scared to 'let anybody in'. That's how River puts it. I hope she doesn't blow it."

"Ohhh… I know that look. You have a crush on your sister's boyfriend."

"Of course not, but according to River, he's a great looking man and he sounds very nice. River says she's already got a *sugar card* from him."

"Sugar card?"

"A card with compliments… sweet words."

"I see. Do you have a boyfriend?"

"No, not since college. I saw a movie, that sort of thing in high school, but if you didn't put out… you weren't asked out again and River would have killed me."

"You dated more seriously in college?"

"One guy for about 5 months, but then he decided he wanted us to sleep together too. I didn't feel that crazy love River talked about, so that was that."

"You work right?"

"Yes, part time. I'm an office assistant and my boss is great. He's a Native American Shaman and a Maze Dancer. He's teaching me a little about sweat lodges, vision quests and things like that."

"Do you like that sort of thing?"

"A lot… It's very interesting. I want to participate in some of those things once he feels I understand enough. He says I have a heart for it."

"It's good to have interests outside of your daily life. You run with that."

"Thanks. I will."

"Back to Ember then. We're pretty much out of time Rain; is there anything else you'd like to say before we stop?"

"Not really. That's about all I have to say about that." She said with a grin.

"Forrest Gump… cute." Echo smiled. *"A sense of humor in all this is good… strange, but good I think."*

Chapter 8

HAVANNAH SAT AT A TABLE near her desk at the Library. She hated that desk, so she made herself accessible close by. She'd been here all day and hardly spoken to anyone. She preferrered it that way; she was quiet and shy. She didn't back away if she was approached, but she didn't reach out either. At 25 she'd been very sheltered, but not by others; she did that herself. There were times when she needed solitude and quiet and the library was perfect.

She hungered for peace of mind... of soul. She had often wondered if there was a God and if He was good, but she knew so many church people and they didn't reflect any God she wanted any part of. She'd read a few books here at the library, but they gave her nothing to cling to. She had already eliminated some other religions, the new age thing, meditation, yoga and even voodoo.

She'd been here all day; they'd be closing in about an hour. Except for the head librarian at the desk, the gentleman at the other end of the table and her, it appeared every one was gone. There may be a few others of course that she couldn't see, but this late it was usually slow. She decided to go upstairs and see if any other books on God could draw her interest. Sooner or later one would help her in one direction or the other.

Her fingers glided along the titles followed by her eyes. She felt no enthusiasm; just a need to find peace at whatever juncture might arise and the answer land in her lap.

"What was that noise? Someone else is up here." Her mind bulked at the idea that she might not be alone. She stood motionless, quiet and listened.

Someone was breathing heavy... and moaning? *"I'd better check. They might be ill."* Slowly, cautiously she moved towards the sound. She peeked around the corner... her eyes doubled in size, her mouth dropped open, her hand flew to her mouth muffling her gasp and she pulled back behind the book shelf.

Her head felt jumbled, she was dizzy; what she had seen wasn't possible. She pulled herself together and braved another peek with the same reaction as the first time. Now she was afraid to move; what if they heard her? Her eyes were closed now, but the vision before them was bold and clear... three men, all naked, doing... Their voices were clear now, as though they had acquired a microphone. She wanted to stop the sounds, but they only got louder.

"Are you for real? You blow my mind. I've never had this kind of relationship before; this is freakin' me out."

"Freaking **you** *out!?!?"* she thought. But she found herself looking again. A tall blond stood naked leaning against the wall; his penis protruding out in front of him. A dark man; hairy everywhere (*it was gross*) knelt before him and the penis was being pushed down his throat. A third man on his knees behind that man, big, husky like a wrestler; he was ramming his penis in the man's... *oh my god...* ass; in his ass. There was grunting and cussing, though muffled, as they tried to be quiet, so as not to be heard downstairs. They didn't know she was there.

"Baby I am for real. We are for real and when I cum I'm going to suck you dry."

She pulled back, blinking her eyes, covering her ears, but it was too late. The image, the sounds... she had to get out of there. Slowly, softly she backed up a couple of rows before she turned and worked her way to the stairs.

"God... if there is a god, please don't let the stairs squeek."

She was too shaken to gather herself and walk out. Her knees were weak and she still felt dizzy. She sat back down at the table. The man at the other end took one look at her and came to her side.

"Are you alright? Can I get you some water or something?"

She could only nod.

He came back with the water and sat down. "Can I do anything else? You are rather pale."

"Aahhh… no, I'm okay, really. I just…" her words fell away.

He didn't move, her breathing returned to normal. At last she looked at him and blurted out, "Do you know god?"

"Know God?"

"Yes, you know; the god of the bible."

"Oh, well yes; I believe I do."

"Is he real?"

"I believe He is."

"What's he like?"

"What do you think He's like?"

"I've read a little. The books call him the trinity. You know… the father, the son and the holy spirit. What does that mean? I read that the father is the boss with all the power and wisdom and this Jesus is his son; always happy and nice to everyone. The books say he died for us, but I don't get that."

"That's not so far off. By the way, my name is Josh; and yours?"

"Havannah."

"Well Havannah, you're a lovely young woman, so let's see what I can tell you. God the Father created everything that we know and everything that we don't know and He loves us. He has the Power. He lives in Heaven, full of wonder and beauty. He wants us to be His family and live there with Him when we go on to our next life, but He can't have bad things or bad people there."

She balked slightly.

"As humans we've all done bad things, so we need to be disaplined to teach us to be good." Josh continued.

"Like parents should do with their children?"

"Yes, but He doesn't want to punish the whole world, so Jesus came to earth to be punished for all of us. He was never bad, so His perfection cleansed us in the eyes of God."

"How is it that Jesus could suffer for us when it's our crime?"

"Like a mom that sees a man with a gun going to shoot her son for hitting his child. The boy is guilty and he would die, but guilty or not, she loves him. Because she loves him, she steps in front of him and takes the bullet and dies for him."

"So why didn't god the father just take the bullet for us? Why send the son He must have loved?"

"He did in a way, for He and Jesus are one."

"Too much to comprehend now. What about the holy spirit? The books make it sound like she's the mother god. She comforts and teaches like a mom; cept she's like a ghost mom."

"Now that's too much for me." Josh said. "I need to study on that and get back to you. Can we talk again? I come here often."

"I'd like that Josh."

"I think they're closing. Can I walk you out?"

"Yes." She didn't want to take the chance of being alone if she saw those men again; she was sure she'd faint.

****

Havannah went home and River sat waiting for her; it was like he knew she had something to tell him and she did. She told him everything... the three men, Josh... their talk about god. She always told him everything and he always told everything to Rain. Rain was his favorite. Havannah knew that, she didn't care. River listened to her when no one else did.

****

Havannah went by the library the next day, but Josh wasn't there. She meandered around a while and then went to the movies. She liked going alone; she could drown herself in the plot and be free of all thought. She caught the last bus home, but the full moon enticed her when she got off at the bus stop. She headed down the path that led through the park. The moon was full and there were lights along the way though very far apart. The trees thinned out about half way and she sat on a nearby bench to gaze at the stars; it was her 'calgon-take-me-away' plan.

Silently he slipped up behind her and kneeling he wrapped his arms around her. He covered her mouth with one hand and held the knife to her throat with the other.

"I love you." He whispered; his voice raspy with emotion. "You have done well, you've offered possibilities for thought and your work is done now. You are not needed anymore. Now you will rest."

The pain lasted less than a split second, she felt the warm dampness as her blood flowed from her neck, she choked and it was over. He held her, he cried and he was gone.

****

Sage was out doing errands when she saw a semi-handsome man in his early 30's, sitting in his long, pointy-nosed Corvette convertible with the faded black cloth top. It was torn; faded duck tape held the back window together. He was waiting anxiously for the light to change. He looked at her as though he thought she'd melt into his arms because he was driving a convertible. Her thoughts were simple and straight forward. *"You're not driving a chick magnet idiot; that's a chick's car. It should belong to a poor wild college pussy trying to snag a rich one. She of course, like you, is not smart enough to realize that the car won't do it... nor will the pussy."* She was annoyed with herself. Why she was even bothering to think about all that was beyond her. She simply shook her head as he revved the engine and sped away.

She finished her errands early and decided the fancy bar downtown at the Hilton was the perfect place for happy hour. The next thing she knew it was 8 o'clock and Ross... 5'10", blonde curly hair and big brown eyes, 34 to her 19... was leading her into an extreemly nice room upstairs. Double doors led out to a small patio over looking the small city she hated. A king size bed was pulled back with mints on the pillow. A TV, larger than she'd ever seen, was facing the bed, but there were also two recliners between the bed and the TV in case you'd rather watch from there. On the other wall was a fire place, a small love seat and a large, thick, elegant rug. To the right was a bar, a frig, a coffee pot, a microwave and a stocked liquor cabinet.

"Mix us a drink while I call room service." He said, kissing her on the neck and walking over to the bed to make the call. After which, he quietly slipped up behind her; while gently kissing the back of her neck, his hand slid up her blouse and softly massaged her breast. His other hand made its way down into her panties, slowly moving through the curls, playing ever so gently with the waiting clit. He nibbled carefully, but firmly on her shoulders, her neck.

She sucked in her breath and held it, relishing his every touch. He turned her to him and his tongue pressed into her mouth demanding control as he grabbed her ass and pushed her pelvis hard against his bulging cock. She rubbed against it with tiny gyrations.

He pulled her skirt to her ankles and ripped her panties off. Then picking her up he bent her over the small table and made his masculinity known by ramming his throbing penis into her wet pussy; claiming her... urging her on, changing the angle until finally he located her place of no return... fucking her until she screamed her final release and then filling her with his hot gushing semen.

He carried her to the bed and removed the rest of her clothes and his. His kisses moved slowly from her naval to her lips, tasting the sweet nectar of her tongue and running his fingers through her hair.

The knock at the door brought champagne and strawberries, cheese and crackers... and ice cream.

They snacked and nibbled and drank champagne... then he guided her to his penis where she feasted until finally he pulled away.

He lay her back on the bed and pulled the ice cream from the bowl of ice; with his hand he scooped and rubbed it on her breast and began the feast of his own, first one breast and then the other. The trail continued to her naval as he licked and suckeled his way down. Spreading her legs, the cold ice cream slid through the curls, past the lips, chilling the tiny clit. The sensations in her body were driving her mad, but they were nothing to what burst through every nerve when he took that clit into his mouth. She squealed with pleasure pushing hard against his face, moving against him; the fire building rapidly toward the explosion of pleasures as the orgasm consumed her.

He moved back up to her breasts his hard cock pushed at the V, but it was not his destination. After a short stop at her bossom he moved on up her body until his eager erection was back between her lips. She teased the tip momentarily and then sucked him as deep as she could and began to stroke the length of him with her lips.

"Oh fuck that's good." He groaned.

Then he matched his strokes with hers as he thrust again and again into her mouth until the warm silky liquid filled her mouth and dripped off her chin.

Ross was her second encounter; the first had left her wanting… she wasn't wanting now; maybe she was in love.

She went into the bathroom and nearly went into shock. Three sinks, two toilets, a shower to accommodate at least 3 people and a tub that would hold two couples easily. Robes were hung on the hooks and a black lace night gown lay folded on the counter… and a blue one and a red one.

She relieved herself, freshened up, slipped into the black night gown and headed out with the intention of enticing him into the bath. She stopped dead staring at the vision before her. Her mind insisting it wasn't real; her eyes calling her mind a liar. He was there on the bed, naked and smiling at her… a drink in his hand.

She, whoever she was, sat next to him… naked with his hand in her crotch. She was smiling at her too.

"Sage," he said. "This is my wife Dorris. She'd like to join us for a while. I've told her how wonderful that pussy of yours tastes and she'd like to see for herself."

Sage remained frozen in place, her mind was screaming, *"Hate him… hit him… kill him. The fucking bastard is not only married, but he wants to share you with his wife. Tell him what you think of him. Tell her she's sick, then get the hell out of here."*

Her mind was right; that's exactly what she wanted to do, but her feet were still frozen to the floor and her mouth could only sputter.

He got up and came to her, kissing her; one hand on her breast and one on her ass holding her to him. He was hard again. Now she was a mannequin; feeling nothing, but when she felt the **'she'**… move up behind her and slip her hand around to her other breast whispering, *"Good girl; this is going to be some good fucking. I'll bet your pussy is wet as all hell."* …Sage snapped. She jammed her elbow into the woman's gut and her knee into his balls. She grabbed her purse, skirt and blouse and left the rest, running for the door. She ran for the elevator and put on her skirt and blouse while she waited; not caring that the night gown hung, showing below her skirt.

In her car she just sat screaming, screaming… wondering if she'd ever stop.

Chapter 9

SESSION 3 WAS ABOUT TO begin. So far Echo was pleased with the openness with which Rain expressed herself. She still felt completely in the dark as to where it all was going; what road should be taken to begin the healing, but it **was** going and she felt confidenat that doors would open for both her and Rain.

"Let's begin where we left off. Is that alright with you?"

"Of course; whatever you think best."

"Who is next then?" Echo asked.

"Havannah... she is 9 years younger than I am. She is the sister that died 5 months ago."

"I'm sorry Rain. Are you up to this?"

"Yes."

"Go on then."

"Havannah was quiet, a loner. I hardly ever saw her. She spent most of her time at the library. Sometimes when I was reading or just sitting in the yard alone she'd come and sit by me. We spoke very little, if at all, but she seemed to know that just sharing the silence helped me. River never told me much about her; just that she didn't have a boyfriend and she liked to read. He said she was seeking something spiritual in her life and just before she died, she met someone that might have helped her find it... or at least eliminate it as not being what she was looking for."

"Did he say what or who that was?"

"No. I asked him that too, but he said if I wanted to, I should go to the library and look to see if the answer was there. Who ever she met, she met at the library."

"And did you go?"

"I did. I had no idea what or who I was looking for, but I went. I took a book off the shelf and sat down and just waited. I went whenever I could for almost two weeks. I was about to give it up when this man came up to me and said, *"Havannah, how good to see you again. I was beginning to think you'd changed your mind."*

"I'm sorry sir; I don't know you. I'm not Havannah. She was my sister."

"Oh my, the resemblence is uncanny. Are you twins?"

"No, she was much younger than me, so I'm flattered."

"Excuse me... I just realized you keep saying was. Has something happened to her?"

"My sister was killed about two weeks ago."

"Oh, I'm so sorry. That would have been right after we met. My condolences Miss...?

"Hardecky... Rain Hardecky."

"May I call you Rain?"

"Sure, that's fine... and you are?"

"Josh. I met your sister here one night and she asked me about God. We talked a little, but they were closing, so we agreed to meet here again sometime and talk more."

"River said she had met someone, but he didn't know who. He told me what Havannah had said about god just before she died, but I thought she'd read it in a book."

"River?"

"Our brother; my sisters tell him everything and I guess I'm his sounding board because he always shares it with me."

"I see. Do you have any interest in investigating God?"

"I never thought about it, but if it had possibilities of helping Havannah... maybe it could be of use to me."

"Do you have some time tonight? I have come prepared."

"I do have a couple of hours, but I'm afraid you'll have to do most of the talking. I'm sort of just on a fishing expedition here."

"Well then, let's go fishing." He smiled.

She liked him. She had no idea if she was going to follow through with this after tonight, '*but let's see what Havannah was up to.*' *She thought.*

"In our heads we learn that God is good, perfect they say and He is loving. He is forgiving, shows us grace and wants to meet our needs. That's the word they put out on Him anyway. My pastor says only in Him is there 'peace in chaos' and 'joy in sorrow'." Josh said entheusiactly.

"That's what they say, but is it true?" Rain asked. *Was she challenging him?*

"Life happens and we ask in anger and frustration... why? Where was God when my child was suffering? Why was that child left fatherless? Where were you when I needed work? Why couldn't I have a normal family life? Why did you let the child molester, the killer, the theif get away? Where were you when the Great Saddness was smothering me; when I felt despair; when I felt defeated... alone? We feel like saying, '*I'm done God. I'm tired of trying to find You in all this mess.*' But even when we feel that way, we hope He won't let us go. Even when we're not sure there is a God... we hope the stories are true."

"Never thought about it, but it's kind of true. I've felt that way, but it's been years since I even considered whether there was a god or not."

"God wants to bring us up to His level, but to do that, He needs to come down to ours."

"It's hard to picture a deity living like a normal flunky." She said, feeling self-consious. She rarely talked to anyone other than River and her boss, Quake.

"Imagine for a moment... God the Father; tall, well built, about 65 years old. His clothes are casual, but have the look of being expensive. His hair is silver grey and he is clean shaven. He wears a bold happy smile."

She closed her eyes and tried to invision it. "Done." She said.

"Good, now imagine God the Son appearing as a Hill Billy from the Ozarks, though highly educated. He also wears a bold friendly smile. His eyes light up his face as they twinkle with glee. He is called Joshua."

"Like you."

"But do not confuse me with Jesus. I will disappoint you. Now God the Holy Spirit appears as a dainty beauty with soft flowing hair; feathery. She seems to shimmer in the warm light of her smile. Though dainty, she is not weak and in spite of her softness, you cannot mistake the strength she emits. Her eyes fill with compassion, her touch tender, her voice powerful. She is Salena."

Rain's eyes closed again as she brought this unlikely three into her minds eye.

"Now you are there with them, confused and unsure. You think you should talk to them; after all, everyone says talking to God is important. You feel obligated, but don't know what to say. Then Joshua leans over and whispers in your ear, *'No brownie points for talking to dad because you feel obligated. If you have questions... ask them. If you want to say something... say it. Nothing more; nothing less. Dad knows that the tragedies of life, the sorrow and the pain; it causes a gulf between us. There is no easy answer to your pain... no magic. It takes time, and when you get to know us better and learn to trust us... that's when the burdens begin to get lighter.'"*

She sat silently, trying to obsorb it all; feeling a need to make sense of it.

"Rain, young lady, I can almost hear your head spinning. I think that's enough for tonight. Sleep on it and if you want to talk more, I'll be here every Wednesday or Thursday in the late afternoon or early eveining. It would be my pleasure to spend more time with you."

"Alright, I might like that." She got up to leave; he helped her with her chair.

"I meant to ask you..."

Rain looked at him questioningly.

"About Havannah; what happened, how did she die?"

She composed herself and pulled together the 'what ever it was', that helped her speak the tough things in her life and said, "She was killed. She had taken a walk in the park and someone cut her throat."

Echo could not completely control the gasp of shock as Rain spoke the words that ended her sisters story. "Rain, I'm so sorry. I had no idea. She died the same way as Snaper?"

"Yes."

"I understand now why your brother is concerned. By the way, the gun lessons and target practice; how is that going?"

"Fine, turns out I'm pretty good with a gun. Not fast, but if I take aim carefully I do okay."

They were both grateful for the quick change of topic that helped release the tension of the heaviness that was beginning to cover them like a cloud over the mountain top.

"Tea or coffee? Could you use a short break before we move on?"

"Some hot tea would be nice if you have it, but then I'd just like to continue. I want to be normal; the sooner the better."

What Echo said was, "What do you take in your tea?" What she thought was, *"She is so confident that all her bad emotions will be gone and her life completely normal; what if I can't make that happen? What if I fail her?"*

Settled back sipping on her tea she went on.

"Blaze is 10 years younger than I am. She's strong and independent. She loves to go out hiking in the wilderness for hours; sometimes she'll go for 2 or 3 days. She's been doing it since she was 10. She used to get in such trouble being gone so long. Now she carries a gun. She's so beautiful and men fall all over her, but she brushes them off. She says when she's ready and she meets him, she will know right away."

"How do you and Blaze get along?"

"It's like with all of us girls; we just don't share our lives much with each other. We are all so different, but it seems like there is some sort of connection... however small, that I have with each of them. They help me somehow and with Blaze, it's no different. She always seemed to know when my mind or my life was in turmoil; when I couldn't find clarity or peace. At first, she'd just tell me how it made her feel when she was out in the wilderness and I liked to hear her stories. Then one day, when she was 12 and I was 22, she came into my room and pointed to a pair of hiking boots. I put them on and she took my hand and led me to the foothills on the edge of town, just 2 miles from home. We hiked up those hills for nearly 2 hours and then we sat down and watched the sunset. For the first time, I felt what she felt; maybe not as strong, but the peace just seeps into you somehow. With the last of the rays sinking, the dusk was turning into dark and we had to hurry to get back. I've walked those foot hills a lot since."

"You can see peace in your face when you talk about it." Echo smiled.

Chapter 10

BREEZE WAS PREPARING FOR ANOTHER night of fantasy. She was wishing it could be with Jessie, but her fear and determination had ended that possibility. Tonight there would be a new bar... a new hunt. She checked the mirror one last time to make sure that Alice in Wonderland was perfect. Her bags with the Mad Hatter costume were in the truck along with her regular clothes, a stuffed Cheshire cat, a white rabbit, a variety of props and a tape with the Queen screaming "off with their heads".

She passed the bar where she had met Jessie; why had she done that? It was not on the way to her destination. 30 minutes later she found herself sitting at the bar... where she had met Jessie, and hoping. She could not help herself; she had circled 9 times before she finally parked and went in.

She wanted to look around, to look for him, though she was supposed to be looking for her next victim. She was afraid to look either way, so she sat quietly trying to let the music fill her mind.

"Can I offer you a cup of tea my dear? We're so glad to have you here at our un-birthday party." The words were being whispered in her ear and his scent was filling her nostrils; her heart was pounding... Jessie!

His fingers were gliding down the length of her arm until... his fingers, intwining with hers, he clung to her. She finally found her voice.

"I would love some tea. I thank you, but an un-birthday? What is an un-birthday?"

"It's the day I want to spend with you." He spun her stool around to face him.

"I want to spend every un-birthday with you, but for now I will settle for right now, right here… tonight."

"Oh you will, will…?" But before she could finish he was kissing her, sucking gently on her tongue and when it was firmly between his lips he circled it with his, tasting her, hoping she was feeling just a fraction of what he was feeling. If she was… she would never leave him again.

"Jessie." For her, the sound of his name on her lips sent fire burning through her whole body. For him, the sound of his name on her lips was a promise of things to come.

Tonight, when she had stopped at the hotel on her way, she had set the sceene. The signs pointing to the paths, the daisies leading just past the bed to the bathroom and just inside the door, the fur rug like the one at the last hotel. On that rug they would sit, sipping wine and telling her Hatter the plot that would lead them into the realm of fantasy and orgasms.

"Fairy tale girl," Jessie whispered, "take me away."

She slipped off the stool and putting her hand back in his, their fingers winding together, she led him to her truck. She handed him the bag and he changed as she drove.

The wine waited on ice just inside the door next to the rug, not three steps away. They poured, they sat… and she began her story.

"Alice sat in the grass at the edge of the pond, watching the ducks and wishing she had not forgotten the bread that was still sitting on the kitchen table. Out of the corner of her eye she noticed movement and turned to look. The white rabbit was scampering by and she said quite indignant, "Oh no, I'm not following you again; not this time."

"The rabbit simply turned and winked at her as she scowled. When the rabbit turned and disappeared behind the tree she couldn't help herself; she got up and chased after him again. She hated herself for doing it, when once again she tripped and fell into the hole. As each time before, that soft fuzzy rabbit caught her, sat her down in the mud and hurried off."

"You dirty little rat!" she said. "Why do I always let this happen?"

"She stood looking at the pond that lay within the circle of mud and then at the grass that surrounded the circle of mud. She raised her left foot, pulling it from the mud, she set it in the grass, missing the sandal that lay stuck in the mud. Now with one foot in the mud and the other in the grass, she bent over to pick up the sandal. Her fingers slipped and the sandal sank out of reach. In a huff she pulled the other foot out and put it in the grass leaving the 2nd sandal behind.

"What will you do to me this time?" She thought. And then with a deep breath and a sigh, she accepted her situation. Now heading off in the direction the rabbit had gone, she began her adventure.

"Why does the pond always look like the one I sit next to in the park?" she wondered. She brushed it off, for now, as she had reached the edge of the grass and there were three paths. She needed to decide which one to take. As she looked down the first path, which was made of purple bricks, she heard music. The music was soft and slow and wishy-washy. It seemed to have no spirit and it made her feel sleepy. This was not the path for her.

"She looked down the second path which was made of brown dirt and she thought to herself, *"That is the kind of path my sister would prefer, to take her wandering in the wilderness. I don't want to get dirty."* Says the girl who just pulled herself out of the mud.

Jessie sat mesmerized by this woman. With her words, she created reality. He felt as though he was really in the rabbit hole with her.

"She looked down path number three, which was made of yellow daisies. *"I'm barefoot."* She thought. *"The daisies are not only beautiful, but they will be soft under my feet."* She headed in that direction.

"She was careful to stay on the path, for she had no intention of getting lost; that is, until she heard someone whispering her name.

Jessie jumped in with what he hoped she wanted to hear. "Fairy tale girl... Alice... Alice."

Breeze smiled and went on. "It was soft and beckoning, but it was thundering in her ears"… *a contradiction, like it always was down here."* She thought.

She stopped; looking around.

"Oh my, he's so beautiful." She thought as she watched him standing near the path under a weeping willow tree. He was tall, at least 6 feet and he had blonde hair that curled in ringlets on his head. His hair wasn't really long but it curled around his ears under his hat. His eyes were a deep dark brown; unusual for one with such blonde hair. He was looking at her with tenderness, as though he knew her frustrating predicament and felt sorry for her; yet instead of pity, she saw desire in his smile."

During her description of him, Jessie had moved over and was standing by the bed. His minds eye saw clearly the hanging branches around him, knowing the bed was her weeping willow tree.

"I think he's teasing me… flirting." She thought, with a satisfied feeling in her stomach or her heart or maybe, just her head. *"Here I go again with that 'love-at-1ˢᵗ-sight'."*

His hand reached out toward her, beckoning her to come nearer. As her toes moved to take a step off the path of daisies, out of the corner of her eye, she saw the rabbit. He had stopped and was looking at her intently.

Jessie watched as she stared at the stuffed rabbit and she began to speak. "His paw came up in front of his face and he was pointing a toe or a finger at her and he began to shake it back and forth as if saying to her, *"No, no, no."*

"Now she was angry and she growled at him saying, *"Don't you dare tell me what to do! You tricked me into coming down here again and then you think you can spoil my fun. Well it's not going to happen, not this time."*

She turned away in a huff and looked at her young man. She had put a smile on her face as she turned toward him. "Now that smile was fading for his smile was gone and his beckoning hand had dropped to his side. Did he not want her anymore, she wondered? A tear trickled down her face and her whole demeanor went into a slump."

"I'm sorry." She said. *"I don't usually get angry like that, but that rabbit, he tricks me all the time. Please, please forgive my bad behavior."* She had spoken in gentle earnest, but she couldn't bring herself to look at him.

Jessie was in awe at how she stayed in character and decided to begin his part. He hoped it would fit in as she had planned somehow. He cleared his throat to get her attention and when she looked up at him, he smiled that same beautiful smile. As her courage built, the corners of her mouth moved in a nervous twitch and she smiled back. When his smile grew to light up his whole face, her smile changed to match the look of desire on his.

His hand began to rise until once again he was beckoning her to come to him. As she took that first step off the path her foot came down, but not on daisies... she gasped with a shriek of pain as the goat head thorn sunk deep into her foot.

"She's going to drag this out to torture me." He thought. *"I want her so much and I want her now."*

She pulled her foot back quickly and hopping around on one foot, she grabbed the other in her hand, trying to remove the thorn. She lost her balance and plopped down on her butt... daisies flying everywhere. *She was glad she'd used real daisys.*

The young man started to take a step towards her, but the ground held him and he was unable to move. *"He must have hesitated not knowing for sure what I wanted him to do."* She thought. She began her narration of the story again.

"There were no daisies around the path; only the dirt that her sister would love and goat heads that no one would love. How would she reach this perfect man with the funny hat; this prince that she had instantly fallen in love with?"

"She looked around, for surely there was something she could put on her feet so that she could go to him. If she'd been wearing a petticoat, she could have torn it and wrapped the strips around her feet, but she was not." Breeze looked at him teasingly as she spoke those words and smiled; his eyes became darker with desire, realizing she wore nothing under her short Alice dress.

She continued… "Alice turned to see if she could get back to the pond and try to pull her sandal's out of the mud, but there was nothing behind her but a wall of trees. She looked back at her young man to assure herself that he was still there. That he still wanted her to come to him; he was and he did."

Breeze slowly untied and removed her apron and dropped it into the daisies scattering them. She never took her eyes from his. He never took his eyes from her. She unbuttoned the blouse and took it off. The black lace bra lifted her bosom giving it cleavage, making them look larger and making the bulge in his pants bigger. She watched as he moved his hand to it, grasping it lightly as though it hurt. God how she wanted to go to him, but no… not yet. The "Fairy Tale" could not be altered.

She struggled to rip the blouse and it finally gave way. She sat and wrapped it around her feet as he watched, looking at her strangely and gratefully.

"Oh dear god; now he thinks I'm weird." She thought. However, when she stepped off the path and moved towards him, all that remained in his eyes, on his face, from his demeanor… was eager desire.

As she neared, her hand reached toward his and their fingers touched; it was like bolts of electricity traveling up her arm into her bosom and down between her thighs. She sucked in her breath as his other hand reached her waist and pulled her to him. His lips met hers, his tongue probing between them; she eagerly took it into her mouth.

The kiss was long and passionate; the desire escalating between them. Then the kiss was over and he pulled his head back and looked at her. "Woman, what is your name?" He asked. *A full blown smile stretched her lips. He was playing the Fairy Tail to even more extremes, for her.*

"I am Alice." She whispered; her voice so husky with the need of him, she could barely speak.

"Alice… there is un-birthday cake to your left and tea to your right, all awaiting the other guests. But here, where we stand, is a blanket in the leaves under the tears of this weeping tree. In which direction shall I take you?"

"Take me down into the soft fur of the white rabbit. There you will take me up into the heaven's of perfection with your touch, with your eyes… with your power that is pushing against me, eager to find the secret places that are inflamed at just the hope of it."

"I see tonight it is you who are the silver tongued devil." He grinned.

"A silver tongue I may have, but it speaks the truth."

There were no more words… discernible words anyway; only moans, grunts and squeals of pleasure, accompanied by biting both soft and hard… kisses deep and wet… soft carresses and deep massage.

There was stroking and sighs and passion beyond description. All of this to announce the orgasms that vibrated through them over and over again.

When the shuddering ceased and the panting subsided, he carried her back to the path of daises that led to the bath. The bath where they bathed each other before he turned her over the side of the tub and they reveled in the sounds of splashing water, wet flesh slapping against wet flesh and the sweet release of yet another orgasm.

They dressed… they nibbled un-birthday cake and drank tea under the shade of the weeping willow and he undressed her again. She lay naked and he fully dressed.

"You are mad," She pouted, "if you think you can keep those tempting parts of your body, that I love so much, hidden from me."

"I wouldn't think of it my dear Alice." He said, as he stood and began to undress before her. Last but not least, he removed his hat and lay back down beside her.

She quickly sat… almost as though she were insulted. He sat too; afraid he'd done something to spoil her fairy tale. She looked up at him, a grimace on her lips.

"My Hatter," she said, "read my lips… My Hatter; there is a reason for that. You will take me with the hat on and it will not fall off. Is that clear kind sir?"

"Yes my dear Alice; quite clear, but it is a very tall top-hat and a bit unstable on my head. What if it should fall in the throes of passion? How would I controll that?"

"If you want me, if you need me... if you are the man I need you to be, you will maintain control even then."

"But how do I kiss you; if I do, the hat will fall."

"The kiss is treasured, but not required for the success of either your fountain... or mine."

"Oh that silver tongue again... I accept your challenge."

There was no romance here, there was rising passion, but mingled with squeals of laughter, playful giggling and sudden stops to maintain hat balance... and then victory, as the switch was flipped and the fountains exploded and they remained locked together, his manhood firmly inside her until the giggles faded away; replaced by gentle caresses and the tender eyes of romance.

On the way back to his truck she was suffering. The more she wanted him, the more she needed him, the more she felt she loved him... the more she knew it had to end. There was no 'happily ever after' in this life. Her life had proven that. A fairy tale was just that... a fairy tale that could only end badly in real life. Again she denied him her phone number... she went home; alone.

Chapter 11

"Good morning Rain. How was your weekend?"

"Good morning Quake. It was fine sir; nothing special or out of the ordinary."

"Seems like your pat answer young lady. Are you sure it's not a recording and you just push a button?"

"I don't remember my life ever being any different. I guess it would seem boring to most people; especially you."

"Why do you say that... especially me?"

"Your life is so alive; you have so much wisdom. You understand yourself and you're not afraid of anything, so you feel free to do anything. I'm always leary about life outside of routine. What life I do live is vicariously, though my sisters."

"We need to change that. We've been going to study together for a long time. What say we start now?"

"Now? What about work?"

"I can't think of anything we have scheduled today that can't wait. You need to start living your life. Your life; not your sisters. It's time you jump out into the river of life and let it carry you to the vast experiences and conquests that give you fulfillment, joy, peace and satisfaction."

"Quake Maze-Dancer, you make me feel almost excited just thinking about it. Do you really think I could accomplish all that?"

"Not a doubt."

She wanted this; that's why the psychiatrist, but what if she failed? How would she know if she didn't try? What if she didn't fail? Maybe between Echo McMasters and Quake, she'd have a real chance to feel alive.

"Coffee?" she asked.

"And donuts." He handed her money and said, "You run down and get them. I'll be ready to start when you get back."

She would go to Ember's coffee shop and maybe see her. As she was going in she saw a man in a cowboy hat and boots. He was just leaving and heading down the street; she didn't get a good look at his face. She wondered if it was Ember's new boyfriend. She would have asked her, but she wasn't working.

She could have made coffee in the office, but since she had to come down for donuts it didn't make sense. Her arms full, she knocked on his office door with her forehead. She was really lucky to have such a wonderful boss.

He opened the door for her and with a bow, motioned her in. She set a second cup of coffee for each of them, that they could warm up later, on the micro and placed the rest on his desk.

"Smells good; you ready?"

"As I'll ever be."

"I preach, then we talk, but feel free to stop me anytime to ask questions."

"'K."

"I want you, when you go home today, to sit back with some nice hot tea and think back over your past. If you have time, do the same with your present; if not, plan to do it tomorrow night or the next. In due time, you will use those thoughts to seek your future. I don't want you to see **you** in your past. I don't want you to think 'I' or 'my' past. I want you to stand aside and see each situation as though you were observing someone else's life. Envision the you in the picture as a stranger. Be aware; watch her face, her eyes and body language to see her emotions. See if you can determine what caused those emotions and what effect they had on her, as well as anyone else involved. Can you do that?"

"I can try." She said, somewhat leary.

"That's your homework for tonight. Now let's move on to lesson one."

"Yes, lets." She said, excited for this new challenge to begin.

"Life has many directions. We have to choose which roads to take. Our freedom to choose is a gift that we all to often do not appreciate or even take advantage of. We let people and circumstances outside ourselves dictate how we live. When life seems like a maze, there is a way out. You can't be lost in that maze unless you quit trying to find your way out." He went on barely stopping to breathe.

"Internal problems, the crazy mind spinning, emotionally draining problems can't usually be handled by external means. Your subconscious responds to whatever you meditate on... what you think about; good or bad. It's even stronger than outside influances. It transfers to your attitude and personality, but in time your body will also be effected physically."

"A tree, a rock, a bird or even a blade of grass cannot talk, but it can communicate with you if you stop listening to yourself and meditate on what pleases you... like a passing cloud, a warm summer rain... listen to the wind."

"The first calendar my people ever used was the Turtle's shell; it expressed 13 moons before the return to the first season. We called it the Medicine Wheel. It was sacred. It also represents the skills that we have the potential to develop. It's a 28 day cycle; the real rhythm the Creater gave us."

"When we say we did not ask to be born or have a rotten life, that is a lack of responsibility. It's a lack of gratefulness for the life and free will given us; it blinds us and we cling to it by choice... as an excuse." He never paused. Words just kept flowing.

"The first sound the unborn child hears is two heartbeats together; the mother and the child. At birth we lose that comforting sound. That comfort can be restored in the silence if we listen; we hear the still small voice... sometimes from within us and sometimes from the wind, the past, the future, the Creator... and we know we are never alone."

"The gift of love is the greatest of all. Within it are communication, nurturing, pleasure, sensations, hope, peace, joy... there is an unending list. To reject it, to abuse it, to deny it, to ignore it, to misuse it… is the greatest of crimes. True love, unconditional love, is pure. It is to be respected, trusted, cherished so it can grow… multiply."

"I don't know much about love; I'm not sure I've ever seen it. I think my brother loves me, but even then I'm not sure if that's the love you are talking about." She said with a sigh.

"Rain, I think that's the saddest thing I've ever heard. I'm sure somewhere, sometime you've felt love; it's just buried or forgotten or not truly understood. We are going to correct that along the way here."

"I think I'd like that." She wondered if the warm tight feeling in her chest had anything to do with love.

"Love will last as long as it is cherished. It may grow in a different way from it's origional intent, but it will remain as long as it is cherished. When I feel weak or lost or hurt, I find in my life that in my silence, listening to the songs of nature, life is restored to me."

Rain felt she had added little to nothing to this day and wondered why Quake didn't seem to notice. He continued to encourage her, that she was learning and growing, even if she didn't see it right now.

They had lunch at the dinner down the street and she went back to the office to do some filing. Quake, with some sort of victory grin, said he was going home to take his wife for a drive in the mountains to watch the sun set from their favorite spot.

****

Ember sat across from Task. They had been eating in silence, but he'd not taken his eye's off of her.

"Are you ready to talk to me now?" he asked.

"Think back over your life and talk to me of laughter." She pleaded. "I've never known anyone like you, who possesses so much laughter."

"First my grandpa and now my laughter… are you for real?"

"Please." She pleaded.

"There was the time my sister asked me to let the poor little baby skunk out of the trap. *"It's so little."* She said near tears. *"It's too little to spray. It won't hurt you. Please Task; it's just a baby."* Yeah right! I had to sleep outside for 3 days scrubbing that smell off. I had to wash 3 or 4 times a day. I was sure I wouldn't have any skin left."

Ember was giggling at the way he crinkled his nose remembering the smell.

"Sure, funny to you little miss; you wait for our next day in the woods."

"We haven't had our first day yet."

"Oh, right..." He pondered... *She played her part to the hilt. It confused him, but he liked it... didn't he?"*

"More; tell me more." She begged.

"Well there was the time my gramps told me about the day he ran naked through the forest. I asked him why. He said a coyote had been after the chickens for bout a couple weeks. He was sitten under the trees with his... my grandma to be. They'd finished the picnic and had moved on to more **amusing things** when that coyote wandered by with one of those chickens in his mouth. He said, *"I got up with my flag a flyin' and ran after that scoundral, hurling thunderbolts at it. You can do those things when you're a young pup. Your grandma... she wasn't your grandma yet, but she was laughing so hard I saw that little trickle of pee slip down her leg. I held that over her all her life."*

Ember wasn't giggleing now; she was doubled over with laughter. She couldn't remember ever laughing like that before. It was almost the most amazing feeling she ever had.

She was laughing so hard that Task could not help but laugh to her equal. As they began to catch their breath he said, "That's the most beautiful sight in the world; seeing your laughter dance in the air, floating in my direction. The sound of your laughter dancing in my head is God's gift to me."

"Humm; he believes in God. I wonder if I do."

"Let's get out of here." He said standing, taking her hand, laying a $50 bill on the table and leading her out to his truck.

****

There was a chill in the air, darkness had fallen and she stood on his patio wrapped only in a blanket. The star-lit sky created a warm sense of wonder. She felt him behind her and the patchwork blanket fell slowly to the ground. Quietly he placed soft kisses on the tiny beads that formed on her skin from the chill, on her neck and shoulders.

They had made love just before she wandered to the patio, while he made hot chocolate. He put the blanket back around her and they sipped the hot liquid. Setting the empty cups down, it was his hungry mouth on hers again, skin against skin. She felt it deep down in her netherland between her thighs and he felt her tremor. He backed her inside and soon... the sensations with each thrust filled them with agonizing pleasures. The tensions peaking, the pleasures complete, he nuzzled into her neck. His warm breath relaxing her into total contentment.

She breathed in his scent, binding it to memory, but it was arousing her again. He felt her body twitch and when it did his flacid member did the same. She had never known that anything could be like this; it nearly paralized her with fear of losing this feeling... of losing him. He melted those fears, if only for the the time of the building orgasm and the ultimate release of it.

Morning came and she tucked the pillow behind her back as he handed her the coffee. He crawled back in bed beside her, kissed her cheek and relaxed back with his cup of black, man-coffee.

He didn't look at her, but he began to speak. "Every morning I long to hold you. I need you, I want you, I have to have you... your warmth, your smell, your taste..."

She could hardly breathe now. Could he really feel that way?

"You're hot, wet... extreemely satisfying. You always put a smile on my face."

"This is a bit overboard. What is he really trying to say? Is he teasing me?" Her thoughts were swimming. She had little experience with this sort of thing... actually, no experience.

He rambled on... "You are the first thing I want in my mouth when I wake." He turned to her and she looked up at him. He lifted his cup up to her and said, "Aahhh... Coffee!" And then he grinned.

She was laughing, but she was also hitting him and coffee was spilling everywhere. He took her cup and set them both down, grabbed her and the playfulness in their lovemaking created a new bond between them.

****

River sat at Rain's side at the breakfast table. They were home alone and this was her favorite time. She avoided the kitchen like the plague if anyone else was home.

"Sage said she saw Ember and her boyfriend yesterday." River said casually.

"I thought I saw him a couple days ago, coming out of the coffee shop, but I only saw his back and Ember wasn't there to ask."

"Since Sage had that thing happen to her with that married man she's been different. She's always talking about Ember and Task. It's like she's stalking them, but I can't figure out why."

"Why **would** she do that?" Rain asked, herself as much as him.

"Maybe she's jealous or has a crush on him? Hell, I don't want another problem to deal with."

River's annoyance seemed a little extreem. "It's probably just a phase; Sage is only 19."

"Old enough to act like an adult." He insisted.

"I have to go to work; see ya later."

Chapter 12

"GOOD MORNING RAIN. YOU'RE LOOKING well. Have you been sleeping better?"

"I think I have."

"Well let's get started. This is session 4. Are you ready?"

"I am."

"We still have one sister left… correct?"

"Sage… yes; and Breeze. I don't remember if we talked about Breeze."

"Mentioned I think; tell me about her."

"She's addicted to sex I think. She never dates the same guy more that 2 or 3 times at the most. I love to listen to River tell the stories though. Breeze carries out all her sex fantasies in fairy tales. She never goes on a normal date."

"What do you mean?"

"She dresses up like a fantasy character and goes out and finds some guy to play out the fairy tale with."

"Can you give me an example?" *Echo was intrigued; curious… not sure she understood.*

"Once she dressed up like Cinderella, but she didn't like that guy much. Then a couple weeks ago she played Maid Marian and found two guys. One was Robin Hood and the other was the God of Wine and Passion. River tells it all in such detail… like the last time she went out as Alice in Wonderland and found a Mad Hatter."

She proceeded to tell the entire story just as River had told it to her. "I don't know why she tells him everything like that, but I think I'm glad she does. I like to hear the stories."

"Wow, she really does play it out in detail. How do you feel about your sister living life that way?"

"It's not my life to feel anything about; I just like to hear the stories."

"Not many would be so non-judgemental about a family member."

"It's not my place. When I think about it… about how they all live their lives, if I become jealous or bitter or…; anyway it's better not to think or judge."

"I'm beginning to wonder if this girl should be counseling me." Echo thought, but said, "Okay then, why don't you talk to me about Sage."

Rain took a deep breath, re-directed her thoughts and began. "She's 19 and still in school. I was 15 when she was born. She was 3 days old when River brought her to me; that's when I knew she was born. I had to take care of her mostly, though he got my sisters to help some. I was grateful for the distraction."

"What did you need the distraction from?"

"On the day she was born I was in the kitchen making lunch. My mom had been sick, so I was making us soup and sandwiches. I heard the door slam and someone stomp up the stairs. I turned the fire down and went to look; it was my dad. I saw him turn towards mom's room at the top of the stairs."

"Do you know why he was home that early?"

"I didn't at the time, but he'd gotten fired and I guess he decided to take it out on her. I heard them talking rather loud, so I fixed the tray, hoping when I took it up things might cool down."

"And did that work?"

Rain could not believe that there were tears for her to try to control. She was sure she must have cried at some time in her life, but she couldn't remember it. There were tears now and one escaped down her cheek before she could stop it.

Echo was amazed at the relief she felt at the sight of real emotion. There had been small glimpses of fear, sadness, anger... but they were minimal and rare, to the point she wasn't even sure they were there.

"No. I knocked and opened the door; she turned to look at me and her lip was bleeding. My dad was ramming into her and grunting; he didn't even turn to look at me. His grunts got louder and his thrusts slower and harder; I knew he was done and I set the tray down and ran out. Next thing I heard was him throwing the tray against the wall."

"Then what happened? Did things settle down?" She was fishing; something had brought tears and it was imperative that she know what it was.

"I knew he'd keep drinking and would pass out. All I could do was wait for that to happen; then I could go tend to my mom."

"But...?" *'She wasn't sure how she knew there was a but, but she did.'*

"But he didn't come downstairs. He was screaming at my mom in the hall at the top of the stairs. *"Get your lazy ass down there and get my lunch."*

"Rain will do th..." My mom started to say, but he grabbed her by the back of her night gown and yelled, *"That cunt daughter of yours can't cook. Now get down there and fix me some real fucking food!"*

"By now I was in the hall watching them. He held the back of her night gown so tight it was cutting her throat in the front. I was going to yell up for him to let go, but before I could, he pushed her. I watched her tumble head over heals again and again. I ran... I don't remember running or where I went, but I found myself sitting in the dark at the kitchen table. I wandered through the house, but no one else was home. Later River came in to my room and told me mom was dead."

Another tear trickled down her cheek, but there was no other sign of emotion.

"After the burial... that's when River brought me Sage. He said mama delivered her after the fall; she was 3 weeks early. That little girl was my life. She kept my mind from falling apart. It was cracked, but caring for her is how I held it together. When she started school we grew apart, but on occasion she'd come to me for advice and I felt needed."

"Being needed, it's a good feeling; it can carry us through a lot."

"She doesn't come to me anymore. She goes to River."

"Do you miss that?"

"I accept it." She said with absolutely no sign of emotion. "Recently Sage met this guy and River says she fell in love on the spot, but it turned out he was not only married… he wanted her to have sex with him and his wife."

"How did she handle that?"

"River thinks she's handling it by fixating on Ember's boyfriend. He's really angry with her. He says, *You don't obsess over your sister's boyfriend; not when you know it's your sister's boyfriend.*" I'm not sure why he put it that way."

"Why didn't you ask him?"

"I don't know. I guess it didn't seem important."

"Do you think she's a stalker or maybe she really is love sick for him?" Echo asked.

"I don't know."

"Maybe she's just using him as an escape because she's hurt or shy… maybe just trying to find a way to survive?"

"I don't know." Rain said, shaking her head.

"Then maybe she is just trying to find a way to move in on her sister's boyfriend. How do you feel about that?"

"I think it's tacky, even though I do feel sorry for her. I don't worry about it. I think Ember is in solid."

"What makes you think so?"

"She has what seems to be a well rounded relationship. You know, it's not just sex." She moved on to tell her about Ember and Task just the way River told it to her.

"It seems as though Ember is a very lucky woman."

"I suppose. I've never thought about any of us as lucky; destined, doomed, fated, designed, condemned, enevitable, unalterable. Any of those things, but lucky… I guess maybe."

"Interesting." Echo couldn't comment further; she needed to process first. "What else has been on your mind or in your life of late? Anything you'd like to talk about?"

"Quake and I had our first real talk where he was trying to teach me."

"How did that go?"

"Well... I think. He told me so much and I have thought about some of it, but not at great length and I think I'm supposed to sort of meditate on it or something. My mind just hasn't been able to wrap around it too much yet."

"Take your time. He will understand. Too much too fast is not usually a good thing."

"I feel bad though; he's taking time out of his life for me and I'm not absorbing it like I should. I will talk to him about it though. He makes me feel really comfortable." She got a sheepish look, broke eye contact and looked down into her lap.

"Rain, what is it?"

"I don't think I should..."

"It's alright if you don't, but we're doctor / patient and nothing leaves this room. I don't judge what you say; I only try to understand it and help you understand it. So, would you care to tell me..."

"I wish he was my father." She burst out interrupting. "That's not right; I have a father. It's just that I never thought of my dad as my father, and the only time I see him is if he's pretty sick; then I take care of him, but I don't want to."

"There is nothing wrong with wishing Quake was your father. He's a good man that you respect and you never had a relationship with your father. It's relationship that makes us family... not blood. You may even want to tell Mr. Maze-Dancer how you feel some day. I think he would be pleased to hear of your affection."

"Maybe... some day."

******

Echo was glad her day was over. She prepared her notes for filing and began her dictation. When finished she leaned back, closed her eyes and let her mind float where ever it wanted.

"Holy Shit!" she said sitting up. "Why did you have to go there?"

Her mind was flashing visions of Breeze and Ember and their amazing sexual activity. She had gotten inexcusably aroused while listening to Rain tell the stories. Now, with the visions in her minds eye, she could feel her body in the early stages of a re-run. What the hell was she to do with this; as if she needed more untended sexual needs since her divorce.

She'd had one fling with an older man in high school that contained a number of orgasms. Her college boyfriend however delivered none. Her husband wasn't the greatest, but occasional orgasms was sufficinet in her busy life. Now, at 51, she'd been divorced for nearly 18 months and had not made time for dating. Celibacy was a relief the first few months, but as she adjusted to being alone and felt comfortable in her skin once again, she was finding herself thinking about sex. Her body was warming with those first twitches of arousal sometimes, but with each story Rain told about her sisters, she became more and more in need of sexual release. The tension was even making her crotchety on occasion. "Holy shit!" she burst again. "Cranky would have sufficed. Why did they use crotchety?" She needed new friends that... what the hell, what did her friends know anyway?

She grabbed her purse and stormed out of the office. When she got in her car, thoughts resumed. What made them think the little time she spent with them gave them the right to judge her 'cantankerous' level?

Her car was in the parking lot of the hotel across the street and she wondered if maybe she'd get a bite at the restaurant; the thought of cooking was unbearable. She went in, but as she passed the bar the sign caught her eye. It read...

"Happy Hour"
Hot Wings... Hot Pretzels... Dogs and Chips
Well Drinks Half Price
Bud Light $2.50

"Hot wings." She muttered to herself and turned into the bar. Planting herself on a stool at the far end, she ordered a Bud Light. She looked around until she found the Happy Hour table and headed for it. She wasn't going to be shy; she heaped the plate as full as she could without the contents rolling off.

By the time her plate was empty she had consumed two beers and the bar had filled; even the stools next to her. On her right was a nice couple in their 60's she'd guess. They had greeted her when they sat, but were now deep in their own conversation. On her left was a very attractive young man. He too had greeted her when he arrived and shortly there after offered to buy her a drink, which she accepted graciously. Now he was talking football with the gentleman on his left.

She wondered if anyone would notice if she refilled her plate; then decided she really didn't care and went back and filled a plate almost as deep as the first one. The bartender looked at her as she sat back down. It made her feel guilty enough that she ordered another beer.

The kid looked her way when he set it down and said, "Let me get that for the lady."

The bartender gave her that 'is it okay' nod and she nodded affirmative and thanked the young man.

"That looks really good; is it?"

She picked up a hot wing and moved it to his mouth. He smiled and took a bite. "Mmmmm, that is good. Excuse me." He slipped off his stool and went and filled a plate overflowing like her first one.

She laughed at him when he sat back down.

They struck up a conversation… "Nice weather, I'm a psychiatrist, I'm a banker, you're too young, 32."

"Oh… by the way, I'm Carl."

"Echo, nice to meet you." She said extending her hand.

Another beer…

"Care to dance?"

"Why yes, I haven't danced in nearly 4 years."

"Then it's time you had a little fun." He took her hand and led her to the dance floor.

He was slightly taller than she was, but he held her perfectly… anyway she was wearing heels. His eyes were a soft blue and they twinkled when he smiled; which he did a lot.

"You are a beautiful woman, but you know that don't you?"

"I think I was beautiful once; faded somewhat I'm afraid."

"Not in the least. Your eyes melt when you dare to keep eye contact more that two seconds."

"Do I appear that insecure."

"No, not insecure in yourself. But you are hesitant to consider me a contestant for your attention… don't! You have my full attention. I like you. You are beautiful, sexy… I bet you were a very playful woman once. Someone smothered that… a shame."

"Why would a young, very attractive, self-sufficient man like yourself be wasting your time wooing a woman of my…?"

"Age?"

"Yes."

"I don't see age; I see maturity. You see age and you shouldn't."

"But…"

How old are you… if you don't mind; you don't have to…"

"51."

"My best relationship was a over two years ago, with a 43 year old. We'd been together 2 years when she was killed in a car accident."

"Oh, I'm so sorry."

"Me too; it's life."

He ordered 2 more beers. Then he turned to her, placed a finger under her chin and tilting her face to his, he kissed her.

"*Holy shit… that warm tingle again.*" she thought.

"Oh woman; your nipples are hard aren't they?" he grinned.

"Oh my god." She gasped.

His hand reached over and slid under her suit jacket and his thumb graced her nipple through her blouse, moving back and forth with a light pressure.

Her breath quickly sucked in, stuck and held. She couldn't breathe.

"Echo," he whispered, "breathe… breathe." He was grinning.

She let the air out of her lungs.

"Take me home with you. I want to stop your breathing over and over." He said, his voice dusky with need. "I want you, to touch you... to feel your skin against mine."

"Oh..." was all that would come out of her mouth.

"Is that a yes?" he grinned again.

"I think so." She said, wondering if he could even hear her or if she just thought the words.

"Come on." He said, handing her her purse and taking her hand.

"Come home with me instead." He said when they got in her car.

She nodded and he pulled her to him, his tongue digging deep inside her mouth and his hand digging deep between her thighs.

The possibilities began flashing in her head; she could be an Ember or a Breeze... couldn't she? Would 32 year old Carl want this old body when he saw it naked? She trembled under his touch and knew that come hell or high water, she was going to find out.

Then she was naked, he was naked... she stood in his arms and his huge, yes huge, erection was pushing against her. He picked her up and throwing her on the bed he dove between her thighs where he feasted until she trembled and squeeled as the orgasm shuddered through her. As she lay panting he moved up beside her. She didn't hesitate; her lips moved to his tiny little nipples and turned them into rocks. Slithering on down she consumed him.

"Oh my god woman; you do that well."

He refused to cum like that though for he wanted inside her... he filled her with his manhood and she thrust to meet him over and over until the explosion of pleasures left them wanting nothing... they slept.

Chapter 13

R ain found herself at the library again. She had Echo to help her, but she wanted it all. She thought the more help, the sooner she'd have results and the better she would be. She would continue to meet with Josh and she would continue to meet with Quake. Between Echo, the Christian God and the Indian Creator… someone had to get through to her deep inside; she was sure of it.

"…and God knows everything; past, present, future." Josh continued.

"If that's true, does that mean that our choices aren't our choices?"

"Of course not. It just means that God knows the choices we are going to make. Just because He knows what you will choose and why, that doesn't decrease your freedom to choose. When God says He can set you free, help you, guide you and save you… it doesn't mean He will. You have to choose to believe Him and accept His gift. That is your choice."

"But what about the circumstances of life. How do we control that?"

"Sometimes we can, but most generally we can't. Circumstances of life just are; it is our choice as to what we do with those circumstances… how we handle them and our attitude. When there is a mess in our life, it doesn't matter whose fault it is. The mess is there and it needs to be cleaned up. It works better if all work together to fix it, even if it's not their fault, but when that doesn't happen, it still needs to be cleaned up. Besides, it gives us a chance to learn to work together in love. Life is not about winning or losing… it's about love."

"But sometimes there is no love; at least none that you can see. You begin to wonder if love is real at all." Rain sighed.

"It's sad, but true sometimes. Some are so damaged they don't know how to function, at least in some areas of life. That is one reason that a relationship that has the potential to have that love is so difficult for them. It may be a romantic love, a love of friendship, a love of compassion, of a child… the list goes on and the loss of it or the inability to participate in it is devestating. God works in the choices we make even when we make the wrong choices. Sometimes we embrace fear, pain and power. We face disaster, disappointment, confusion. Our choices at these times can make or break, but even broken we can rise again. We can fashion the ugliness before us into something beautiful with the right choices."

"How I wish I could see any sort of reality in that, but I must believe it's possible or I wouldn't be looking for the answers."

"You speak words of wisdom. Here is a trivia list of more… Evil is the absence of Good. Darkness is the absence of light. Cold is the absence of Heat. Death is the absence of Life. So evil, darkness, cold and death can only be understood within their relationship to good, light, heat and life. We call Him Lord, King, God, but he never takes control of our choices; He never forces us into anything. Grace comes in many facets and shades. Lies are little fortresses you build to make you feel safe from what you 'think' the truth might bring. Now you have to protect that fortress so no one finds out. You make excuses to justify your lies, thus the walls. Now the lie and the walls are inhibiting your choices, your relationships…your future. All that can set you free is the truth. Are you brave enough to face it, to take the chance? There may be a price; there may not, but regardless of the price, the burden of the lie is lifted. You stand tall and free to begin again… a 'do-over'; we all need a 'do-over'.

"I hope you don't mind. I'm taping this. I could never remember it all and it's taking me longer to process it than I thought it would, but I want to try and don't want to lose anything."

"I don't mind at all. It sounds like you have enough to chew on for one night. Next week then?"

"Oh yes, please."

****

Rain knew she'd be overwhelmed doing two teachings in a row, but the next night was the only night Quake could get together for a while and she didn't want to miss it. She'd just tape it and sort it all out slowly. They were meeting at the office at 5:00. She'd stop for coffee and tea incase he didn't do caffeine at night. They wasted no time getting started.

"My people… our teachings can teach much when it comes to approaching life; a way of relating to the earth and to each other. Do not judge yourself by your accomplishments, possessions or how you compare to others in your eyes or anyone elses. Fasting is one way to know things. I told you that when you were ready I'd take you to a sweat lodge to experience a cleansing. Fasting is a preparation for that. When the time is right; I will give you more details and we will go."

"I look forward to it. I told my counselor that you were going to do that with me when you thought I was ready."

"Yes, and I will. We try to find our role in life, and because of it, we can get a glimpse of what it means to walk what we call the Spirit Road. And when we walk on that Spirit Road there is no Catholic, no Jew, no Buddhist, no Indian way or any other special way. Universal love is gathered together on that one road. The caring and love that can generate from our hearts into the lives of others can carry us forward. To walk in beauty we must have a purpose, strive for its fulfillment. All of these ingredients are what give life substance."

He paused to give her a chance to speak or ask. When she remained silent, he went on.

"You must learn to receive as well as to give. Fear is normal, but do not embrace it. If you want to find the silence, so that you can be filled with knowledge and wisdom from within and from above, go to a place where no one's around and wrap your legs around a tree. Then wrap your arms around it, lean your head against it and just be. Sometimes your mind becomes empty right away and the filling can begin. At other times you may begin to think of all kinds of things. Sometimes we let our imagination get away with us. I heard a story about Freud, who smokes cigars, and he simply said, "Sometimes a cigar is just a cigar." Sometimes we have to say that to our imagination. I want you to imagine being like that tree; silent, listening to the world, listening to the wind. Learning and growing unceasingly."

Again he paused and again, she was silent.

"Never claim to know something just because you read about it, heard about it, saw it on TV. You never really know anything for sure, unless you personally have actually experienced it."

"I believe that." She interjected. "I think what I want to know most... I want to know that I know that I know about love; what it is and how it feels. That is my greatest desire."

"And that is the best one. I think with that we should stop."

****

Rain spent the next day overwhelmed and loving it, as she went over and over the lessons she'd heard. She had not had any great revelations from it all, but it only made her more eager to learn... to learn until the revelations came.

The following day she could not shake the sadness that held her in bed. She was filled with trumoil and confusion when, out of the blue, Blaze burst into her room pointing to the hiking boots again. "We're going way up into the mountains; get up... you need this." She was on a mission and as she patted the gun at her side impatiently. "Rain, get a move on."

Far into the mountains... they drove for 3 hours. It was nearly 11:00 when Rain pulled off onto a dirt road as instructed. They continued down that road maybe a mile... maybe not.

"Grab the pack." Blaze ordered.

They walked, they walked, they walked.

"I can't go on." Rain whined. "I need to rest."

"Almost there. Not even a city block; keep going."

Then they were on the river's edge. Rain collapsed on a rock and took off her back pack.

"Take your clothes off." Blaze demanded.

"Why?"

"You're going for a swim."

"You first."

"I'm not going in. You need this, not me."

"The waters cold."

"Take um off or I will."

Obediently she dropped her clothes on the rock in the sun. They were wet from sweat; the sun could dry them and maybe burn away the stink.

She sat on the edge of the rock and dangled her feet.

"Get in."

"It's deep."

"It's only about 4 or 5 feet and you learned to swim in school. Get in."

Rain hesitated.

"Now!"

She didn't know why she was being so submissive, but she slipped off the rock into the water with a gasp. The shock to her body, from the cold water, was worse than she had anticipated. But momentarily she adjusted and it felt exhilarating. She began to swim around. This really did feel good after the long hike. As she floated around on her back she noticed just how beautiful it was and in the silence, the sounds of the woods came to life.

After about 30 minutes she heard, "Get out."

Unquestioningly she did as she was told. She was relaxing and the wretched sadness that had incapacitated her this morning had seeped away. Turmoil of mind, confusion of thought, remained when she allowed her self to think, but she hadn't done much of that grunting and groaning up that mountain. Her mind was clear as long as she stayed in the water. She dressed.

"Here, take the gun." Blaze demanded, reaching the gun out to her.

"Why?" *"Crap, why did I say that? She's just going to give me shit anyway."*

"Because I want to see for myself that you can shoot; that those damn lessons did you any good."

She took the gun and carefully shot at the target Blaze had put up. Four shots... well done.

"Good, now I'm going to throw something... shoot at it. Can you hit a moving target?"

"I don't know, but why do I need to?"

"You're going to have to hunt for our lunch. You have to learn."

"What?!! I can't hunt."

"Are you hungry?"

"Starving."

"Then I suggest you get hunting."

Tears welled up in her eyes. She swallowed and choked back a sob. "I guess I hunt berries then; I can't kill anything."

She heard a giggle. Someone else must be near. She turned to look at Blaze and she was laughing. She'd never seen her laugh before. Her family didn't laugh. And why... why the hell was she laughing at her?

"Relax sister; there's plenty of food in the pack at your feet. Let's eat."

Her laughter subsided quickly as they sat down to eat.

Rain thought that she should have felt relief and laughed with her sister. It was a good joke she'd pulled on her, but she was still in shock.

They packed up the trash and were heading back, but it was unfamiliar; they weren't going the way they'd come. They were walking slower, more leisurely. Blaze stopped and pointed; Rain stopped and followed the invisible line to the deer and her fawn as they lingered there. They watched only a few minutes before the breeze carried their scent and mama deer lifted her nose to the air and they quickly hustled away.

Not far down the path she was again distracted while she watched a rabbit and then a squirrel. They were about half way back to the truck when they stopped to rest. She downed a whole bottle of water and sat on a stump warmed by the sun that seeped through the trees.

She began to think, but instead of the turmoil and confusion that spun in her head that morning, she found that she had one singular thought.

"Blaze, I'm going for a short walk. I want to be alone just for a few minutes. I'll be right back."

If she hadn't had the truck keys in her pocket, she would never have dared do that for fear that Blaze would just up and leave her, but she did have the keys, so she was off.

She only walked a few yards; just enough to be out of site. She looked around and found the perfect one; not too big, not too small, with a bed of dry leaves around it.

She sat, wrapped her legs and arms around that tree and closed her eyes. Thoughts moved through her head; incomplete, single words mostly like... silly, foolish, hide, stop, don't tell... and then... quiet, listen...

At first there was only silence and then, like when she was in the water, the sounds around her became alive... almost too loud. Then slowly they became softer and softer and she felt it... such peace as she had never dreamed possible. She sat there and wallowed in it; wanting it never to end. Then slowly, the wind in the trees began to whisper to her. They weren't discernable, but they were comforting. Soon after the sounds of the woods began to seep back in and she opened her eys... a bird, a bug; she watched until they disappeared.

Back on the trail she had paused to drink more water... the bottle was flying, her feet were kicking and dancing like an Ozark hillbilly. She was screaming at the top of her lungs, as an extreemly large snake slithered between her legs.

The snake gone, her composure returned... she found herself smiling. Quake was right... it's good to hug a tree.

****

At home with River, reliving her day, the peace remained with her. "Your're growing little sister. You're finding answers and learning things... you're healing. I see that you are stronger every day."

"I don't feel stronger every day, but I do today; thanks to Blaze."

Chapter 14

Task had wanted Ember to come over tonight. She told him, only if she could go over right after she got off work. He handed her his apartment keys, kissed her cheek and left whistling.

She grinned; she had a plan. He had a heavy load today… he'd told her so. She wanted to care for him and his needs. She hit the grocery store and picked up dinner. She cooked, though it wouldn't be ready by the time he got home. She showered and slipped into very tight jeans and a low cut blouse, met him at the door with a glass of wine and a kiss; then sat him down and removed his shoes massaging his feet.

"Dinner's not quite ready. I'm running you a bath."

"You serious?"

"Yes." she answered, taking his hand and pulling him up. "Go get undressed. I'll warm it up." He kissed her cheek and went to obey. She tucked him in the tub and handed him a fresh glass of wine. "I'll be up to get you when dinners ready."

It was a hot dinner… home cooked, but light, so as not to keep him from sleeping. When they finished she led him to the bedroom and dropped his robe to the floor. He reached to pull her close and kiss her, but she held back.

"Not yet…" she whispered. "Lay down on your back."

He did and she began at his temples and massaged his body all the way to his toes… arms and fingers not forgotten and his special purpose carefully avoided. It would wait. When she finished she said, "On your stomach." *She had done her research on the massage.*

He was obedient and she felt a twinge of smug. She proceeded to carry out the same loving touches from his neck to his tush to his feet. He fell asleep as she had expected. She covered him with the sheet and softly kissed his temple, so as not to wake him.

She headed down to the kitchen to clean up and then slipped in beside him and watched him sleep. When he began to move around in semi-wakefulness, she snuggled close and wrapped her legs around him. She wouldn't play yet, but she needed to feel his skin on hers.

In the early morning, just before daybreak she woke; they had apparently tossed and turned, for now his beautiful erection was poking her in the back, even though he was still asleep.

She slipped in to the kitchen and came back with her hands full. He had rolled to his back and kicked the sheet off and fell back asleep. She prepared and sneaked back in beside him. She kissed his temple and along his jaw bone to his chin. He was awake now and she stopped there for a long, lingering kiss. Then she gently teased each nipple as he realized there was strawberry juice on them. She sucked and licked his body moving down slowly. She poured warm chocolate into his naval and trailing it down to his ample erection. Then she licked every drop away.

Backing down between his legs she teased the tip of his passion. Moving down, she gently sucked each testicle in her mouth. His response caused the feeling of arousal to flicker through her body. Feeling the prickle and sting of electric pleasure, she moved back up, took him fully in her mouth and began moving with somewhat more zeal. He hadn't touched her, yet the foreplay was complete. She was wet and ready... need making her nipples stand at attention. She could wait no longer.

She moved up and lowered herself over his beautiful hardness gasping in whimpering moans as she covered him... as he filled her. He reached up and pulled her down for a warm, wet, breathtaking kiss; feeling her nipples hard against his chest. It was more than he could bare. His hands moved to her hips and he guided her, thrust up into her, called her name as he filled her with the heat of his passion and she came for him tightening around him again and again.

****

They didn't know they were being watched. Later, Sage would tell River all about it. She would tell him how she had followed Ember to his place and stayed hovering outside the window... watching... listening... planning. Sooner or later he would tell Rain.

****

Josh and Rain hunkered down in the back of the library, so they could enjoy the coffee that she had smuggled in. Their greetings were complete and he'd been talking for a while, but it hadn't peaked her interest yet and seemed to be slipping in one ear and out the other. Thank heaven she was taping it.

"Think of a mobile, like on a crib."

She heard that and was wondering what that had to do with God, he had her attention.

"God is the motor. Your life, your friends, your family, your job, your thoughts, your activities... each one is hanging from the mobile. Altogether the motor moves them in harmony in an incredible dance of being. But then there's the wind and each is different, so each moves differently with the breezes of life. This can still be harmonizing or it can be conflicting in part or all of the aspects of your life. Each choice made because of the effects of the wind makes a different road. If you maintain until the breeze subsides and you come back under the protection of the motor-umbrella, all will be well. If not, then more new roads are created and more choices to make."

"I don't want to have to make choices." Rain said sadly. "I just want to live."

"That's what living is... making choices." Josh replied, matter of fact.

He paused, giving her time to speak, but she didn't so he went on. "Think about this... a relationship between two people is absolutely unique. You cannot love two people the same. You can love one person in many different ways, but never in the same way you love another... **not exactly the same**. Each person is different and the more you learn about each other, the more you experience each other, the greater that relationship becomes; the richer and more varied the colors of that relationship intensify. A mother loves all of her children, in many ways and for many reasons, but she will never love them exactly the same for they are different. And with that young lady, I think we will call it a night. I'll bring the refreshments next time." he grinned.

****

Breeze sat quietly at the bar... tonight they carded her. She had been to this bar only once, many months ago, so she smiled her sweetest little girl smile and handed the bar tender the proof of her 21.9 years.

"Where are you going my pretty?" Jessie whispered in her ear, pulling back the red hood and resting his hands on the shoulders of the red cape.

She had mailed him his costume in advance. Immediately he'd gotten the room and told them to give her the key whenever she came in. Now he was standing behind "Little Red Riding Hood". At the sight of her he became aroused.

"Why sir, I'm on my way to Grandma's house. She has been quite ill and I'm taking her some nourishment. I only stopped for a little refreshment, as I was thirsty." As she turned on her stool to face him she said, "What brings you to this part of th..." The words faded and her mouth fell open. He had replaced the costume she had sent with one that was far more extreme and she couldn't believe he was wearing it. "...of the woods?" she finished, finding her words.

He stood before her in fur head to toe. The paws had claws, the tail was at least 18 inches long and bushy. The mask was a full wolf head with ears and bulging red eyes from which his peeked under; the nose long with bared teeth.

"However would she kiss him?" she thought.

He ignored her shocked face and the loss of words and said, "I'm just here hunting rabbit. It might not be safe here in these woods." Looking around he pointed to 3 or 4 different men that were watching her. "There are many wild animals here in these woods. Where does your Grandma live?"

"Just along that path and through the woods a little deeper."

"Possibly I should escort you little one."

"That won't be necessary; I've traveled this way many times. It's quite safe."

"Then I shall be on my way." The wolf said, hurrying off.

He'd guessed by the costume she sent that it was this theme and he studied the story so as not to disappoint her. Just in case he was wrong, he glanced at several other stories with wolves in them. He hurried off to the room to wait; putting on the Grandma night gown and bonnet over his wolf costume.

She waited 15 minutes, brushed off two suiters, tipped the bartender who was grinning ear to ear, picked up her basket of goodies for Grandma and headed after him.

"Grandma?" she said softly, as she tip toed in the door. "Grandma it's me, Red. I've brougth you some food… and tylenol."

Jessie grinned when he heard tylenol. "I'm here in bed dear. I am quite weak."

Red Riding Hood went to the frig and got the wine and two glasses and picked up her basket and went into the bedroom.

"Oh Grandma." She said. "You do not look well; your color is quite dusky… as is your voice." She added to tease, knowing he was probably quite hard already. "I've brought your favorite; cheese, crackers and summer sausage." She served them both and poured the wine. She had to feed him of course for his hands were paws and his mouth was encased in the mask, though there was an opening for her to push the food in if she was careful.

"Oh Grandma, what big ears you have."

"The better to hear you with my dear." He said, confident that he was well versed in the script.

Another bite and a sip of wine.

"Grandma, what big red eyes you have."

"The better to see you with my dear."

Another bite and a drink of wine; she did love drawing the fairy tale out, knowing he wanted her so badly... and he was well aware of that fact.

"Grandma, what a big nose you have."

"The better to smell those pheromones of yours." It was his turn to tease and let her know that he knew she was horny too.

"Oh my." She sipped her wine. "Grandma, what big teeth you have."

"The better to eat you with my dear." He threw the covers back, knocking the basket of food everywhere. He jumped out of bed as she jumped back and screamed. He threw his bonnet and tore off the night gown and snarled and growled his best wolf noise; then howled for all he was worth.

He crept toward her and she stepped back... this went on slowly until she was against the wall. He grabbed her cape and ripped it off. This time it was he who stopped and let his mouth drop open. She was stark naked under the cape.

He carried her to the bed and lay her on her back. He caressed her whole body using his tail like a feather. He moved slowly growling just under his breath, deep in his throat.

She needed no foreplay for she was wet and ready. Even though it was driving her mad, if he stopped she would die. As his tale toyed with her breast, they became more taut and she tensed with need. As he neared the V, she opened to him, gasping and pushing against his tail as he teased also, her taut tiny toy.

He pulled her knees up and opening them wide, he burried his long cold black nose between the lips and played there a while.

Then he moved up her body on all fours. As he hovered over her, he released the flap that covered his tools and his manhood burst out, his testicles falling behind.

There he took her like a beast all in fur, head to toe; stuffing his nose between her lips in place of his tongue. He took her like that from the front, then turning her, he took her again... doggy style. She was on her thrid climax when he finally release his own fireworks.

He collapsed beside her. They were laughing as he said, "Please Red, can I take it off now. It's so hot I might pass out."

"Jessie, I'm so sorry. Of course… let me help you." She said, as she pulled the head off. He was covered in sweat. She helped him out of the rest of his costume and kissed him. Then tasting the sweat from his chest… she let him hold her there. After another kiss she collapsed into his arms.

"The costume I sent would have been cooler, but thank you for getting this one and doing this for me. You are my wildest dream; my greatest fairy tale." She purred.

"It was my pleasure Red; you are my pleasure… from the moment I met you. You have bewitched me and I hope you never forget the spell you used." And as an after thought, he asked, "Is there a witch fairy tale?"

"In due time…" she grinned.

"What say we shower and start over?" he said jumping out of bed.

"Your wish is my command… oohhhh, one day we do 'I Dream of Jeanie'." She grinned.

"Shower together, but no nookie. I need a rest."

She grinned and led him to the shower.

Rested and refreshed they did indeed begin again… no fairy tale; just Breeze and Jessie. They lay sipping Disaronno and whispering sweet nothings.

He pressed his body against hers and she wiggled tight into his arms. Then she was kissing her way down his body, stopping to tease his nipples as she caressed his cock and balls; feeling him get hard. She wanted him to just relax and enjoy. She sucked him into her mouth and felt it throb against her tongue. Wrapping her mouth firmly around the shaft, she began moving up and down on it. Faster, sucking harder, she took as much as she could. Her mouth wet and warm caressed him. She moaned as she felt the arousal and pleasure seeping through her body just from giving him pleasure. She tugged gently on his balls as she tasted his pre-come. Her tongue was lashing as she moved over his cock. She wanted to feel his release, but her own need was intoxicating, building rapidly. Straddling him she guided his need along the slit and the head slips into the wet warmth deep inside. She moaned, taking him all the way inside her. She is motionless, absorbing him. Then she begins to ride slowly. He whispers her name softly… "Breeze, oh god girl."

Bracing herself on his chest, she rides; nipples hard, breasts bouncing, face flushed. She leans back a little more, feeling the fullness of him rubbing against the secret places inside her. His hands on her hips, he thrusts upward, pushing as deep as he can. His fingers are digging into her derrière as they ride rhythmically, faster and faster. Breeze moans louder, she begins to shudder, tightening around him deep inside her; the spasm shakes her whole body and he feels her cuming. His deep husky moans from deep in his throat announce his pending orgasm. He explodes and fills her with his warm silky pleasure. She collapses on top of him, her legs like jell-o.

They slept late, rented movies, took naps and made love; all of which they did over and over. They bathed together leisurely. They burst into sudden torrents of passion. They explored and tasted every inch of each other's body and all too soon the fantasy was over.

****

Rain was standing in line at the hamburger place when someone, not-so-accidentally, bumped into her.

"Oh, I'm sorry ma'am." He said. "How clumsy of me; please excuse me."

That began a pleasant conversation about the weather, the smell of greasy french fries and the terrible service. They came to an agreement that they should go somewhere else more pleasant for lunch. When they got outside, the sun had disappeared and there was a soft, gentle, warm spring rain. On the way to his truck they both got quite wet; he caught himself staring at the cold, pert nipples poking visabily from beneath her blouse. He thought, "*I think they're looking at me with puppy dog eyes.*" He smiled to himself. She was doing it again and he was determined to play the game.

"By the way, my name is Dalton."

"Rain, how foolish that we hadn't already introduced ourselves. I feel silly."

"Rain? Pun intended? No pun intended? Is that a weather report or is that your name?"

"That wet stuff is a co-incidence. My name is Rain."

"If nothing else this woman was unique." He thought.

They picked up food from Blakes and drove to the park just outside of town. All the while she is thinking, *'What am I doing? I don't pick up with men like this. This is just crazy.'* Yet, for whatever reason, she didn't turn back.

The picnic tables were enclosed and protected from the rain. It was exceedingly warm in spite of the rain, so when they finished eating they decided to take a short walk. They walked down the dirt path, leading them deeper into the trees.

Rain's mind was spinning a bit. Four hours had passed since they 1st met and they had been talking nonstop. Going anywhere with a man she didn't know was so unlike her. She was straining to figure out why she had risked going with this man. She was not comforted by the gun in her purse, but she didn't feel the fear and anxiety that she'd always felt before. This man felt comfortable, safe.

Dalton's mind was tinkering with his thoughts too. She held a warmth like he'd never seen and yet a sadness that was overwhelming. It was almost like she was two different women. He was drawn to her like a magnet; his need to comfort her and see her sadness disappear was consuming him. What part was she playing here? Was the sadness a real part of her?

The next thing he knew he was kissing her and the flames, that had lain within her for so long, burst into an inferno.

She'd never felt it before, she couldn't explain it; it frightened her, it excited her, it thrilled her and she couldn't stop it. Clothes were falling to the ground, in the mud, as they stood clinging to each other, becoming naked in the rain.

Dropping to the ground, there was groping and sounds of passion and thrashing in total uncontrolled abandonment as their bodies slammed together in the puddles, splashing muddy water everywhere. The climax for both of them was pure exultation; pleasures thundering through space and reverberating back into their bodies. *Rain was no longer a virgin; it had been painless. She lay reveling in her first orgasm.*

Peeking through the trees to check for people watchers, he carried their clothes back to the truck and threw them in the back. Then pulling two blankets from behind the seat, he wrapped one around her and turned the heater on. He new the reality of the pleasures they had just shared. The look on her face was euphoric, but the sadness remained in her eyes. Was this real or...?

The pull was as strong with this woman as it was with the others. It was different yes, but equally strong. He couldn't leave her like this. He wanted them all... he had them all.

"Can you stay with me a while longer? We could get a room and send our clothes out to be cleaned and order dinner in. I don't want you to leave me yet. I wish to know you more deeply."

There was panic at the thought of it, there was eagerness to comply; there was the need long unfulfilled and a place untouched within her that he was healing. She could only nod. *All of this... it's so strange and intoxicating. I've never done anything like this before. Why haven't I?'*

The busyness of their plans past and they lay side-by-side under the covers. He held her. Would she let him explore the wonder of her... without another moments hesitation, he began to search out and learn her entire body as if he'd never touched her before. His fingers and his tongue moved inch by inch, gently teasing each of her nipples and her belly button. His tongue would find her warm wet cave and slowly it would part the lips and touch the tip of her clit, ever so gently. He lingered there for what seemed to her a lifetime... a perfect lifetime. Slowly his tongue moved to penetrate deeper inside her. She felt that every nerve ending, that could ever find pleasure, was right there drinking up his touch.

When his fingers and his tongue had covered her all the way to her toes and back, he penetrated her silky dark cavern. Moving gently at first, but with slow firm strokes. Each stroke became more deliberate until she received all of him with heart pounding thrusts. Her limbs quivering, they came together and he held her.

They lost all track of time, just enjoying the closeness of each other. They would fall asleep, arms and legs wrapped around each other; then they would wake finding that it was not a dream. When finally no time was left and there was no choice but to part ways, he took her back to her car.

In the aftermath, on his way to work, he ached to have her back in his arms. He would call her, surely this new one would see him again… she did give him a phone number. They were so different and yet somehow so much the same.

****

Quake took Rain to a Pow Wow. They watched the dancers and he explained the different dances. She scarfed down all different kinds of Indian food and she bought a dream catcher and a pair of earrings. He explained that the dream catcher could be hung any-where, but was most often hung above the bed or in a window. The idea was that if bad dreams came they would be caught in the web and at the first light of dawn the sun would burn them away. When the good dreams came they could slip through the hole in the center to those for whom the dream catcher was bought.

As they shared dinner, in the late afternoon, he told her of other things. "Many of us are people watchers and observe others; their actions, their behaviors, their attitudes. We could learn from that, if we could learn to observe without judgment." He paused. "Next time you go to the zoo, stare at the Tigers."

"I've never been to the zoo."

"Oh dear, we have a lot more work to do than I thought."

"Not to worry," Rain said. "I will go to the zoo."

"Not the point, but another time. Have you ever tried to sit still for just 20 minutes?"

"No."

"Try. Don't move at all."

Two minutes later she sighed and Quake said, "Don't sigh, don't scratch your nose. If you begin to feel stiff, don't streach. Remain expressionless no matter what you see."

Sixty seconds hadn't passed when her nose began to itch. Then she was thrsty, then she got a cramp in her foot and before long she saw a man back-hand his kid. She couldn't do it. All those things had taken place in the matter 4 minutes.

He laughed at her and said he would explain in more detail the self-disciplinary rituals; another experience that maybe one day, she could partake of.

"My people learn from the seasons, the things that grow, the animals and many other life forms. After that we tried to learn the things that are within ourselves. We will never know every thing. We spend a life time learning and then saying things like... Been there; did that. We can't just learn things to be within us. Yes, it helps us be us inside, but we need to learn to express without... Contentment, victory, joy, laughter, love, peace, satisfaction. These things are not just things that we need within us, although we do; we need to be able to express them as well; and to see them in others."

"Quake, how do you remember all this; it's so overwhelming."

"You will remember by living... one step at a time. And as you remember the steps behind you, those in front of you will be easier. One last thought... be aware and understand the ways of evil and you will be more able to stand against it and be victorious over it. And with that, I think it's been a very long day. A very good day, but a long one just the same. Let me drive you home."

Chapter 15

Echo began to set the room up for session 5 with Rain. She was being drawn into this woman. She wasn't sure if it was going to make it easier to help her or if she should be afraid of getting too intertwined. She'd given it a great deal of thought and had come to the conclusion that it didn't matter what the outcome... she was in this for the long haul.

"I had a dream last night... confusing, strange." Rain began.

"Tell me about it."

"I woke up groggy, but I remembered the dream clearly. I was sitting in an office with some lady who was inquiring about me and my family, but I don't remember why. I told her everything... all about us and it took hours and hours. Why was she so nosey and why did I agree to do it without asking questions? I guess it doesn't matter; it was just a dream, but I do believe dreams mean something. I just don't have a frickin clue what. Finally, I just shook it off and headed for the shower."

"Doesn't that sound familiar to you?" Echo had never heard her even hint at a cuss word before.

"I don't think so."

"I am some lady, we are in my office, I ask you multiple questions about your family..."

"Holy Crap! I'm such an idiot. But why would I dream about it?"

"That I don't know. It might just be overload; it might be you're rethinking about going on. Have you thought about discontinuing our sessions?"

"No, not even a little. The thought never crossed my mind."

"Maybe your concerned, unknowingly, that you have forgotten something that your subconscious thinks you should tell me. Just give it some time. If it's really anything of significance, it will come to you."

"Alright."

"So what else is new?"

Rain got a little excited. "So much this time; I don't know where to start. Let's see... my Indian boss, Quake, took me to a Pow Wow and told me to hug a tree."

"Hug a tree... that sounds interesting. Is there a purpose in that?"

"Yes."

"I guess she's not going to tell me what that purpose is. I'll wait."

"And did you... hug a tree?"

"I did, yes... see this one morning I was a mess; I didn't even want to get out of bed. Blaze came in and we went to the mountains. I've never felt the way I felt that day. She made me swim in the river and shoot my gun. I saw a mother and baby deer, a rabbit and a squirrl. I hugged a tree and watched a bug. Oh my God, it was amazing... even the snake."

"Snake?"

"On the way home this snake crawled between my feet. I was scared to death... screaming and all, but after, when I calmed down, I discovered that I loved that too."

"I don't know if we're any closer to finding out why you are here," Echo said, "but we certainly are closer to your being well. I seldom see you this excited about anything."

Rain squirmed and smiled nervously, relishing the words, encouraged by them yet still uncertain in her own skin.

"It's funny that you say that now. River said much the same thing to me a few days ago. He says I'm healing and stronger. I think it might be so, but I don't feel as strong as you two seem to think I am."

"It will come."

Rain told Ember's story of what, to her, seemed like... 'pure love'; at least the way River told it to her. Then she told her what River said about Sage following them and spying on them. River said, *"When she was telling me about it, guile dripped from her words. I'm a little afraid of what she might do; guile is not a logical thing."*

Echo was amazed that her brother was so on target with this... guile definitely was not a logical thing and it could be dangerous. It could turn into something quite ugly, but she did not interrupt... she just let her talk on.

"Breeze and Jessie had another fairy tale. I think I'm starting to get a little jealous, but I could never do any thing like that."

"Don't worry about that; I think I'm a little jealous of her free spirit too. What was the fairy tale this time?"

"Little Red Riding Hood." She told her the details of Breeze's story with as much enthusiasm as she had Blaze and Ember's.

"There's something else you want to tell me isn't there? You're holding back, why?" Echo asked.

"Well, I don't know what you'll think. I don't know what I think and I'm a little afraid if I say it out loud, it won't be real; just some part of my imagination or wishful-thinking overload."

"But whatever it is, there is a smile that is fighting desperately to cross your face and you're not letting it. A couple of times I thougtht you were going to just start grinning and hug yourself. It must be a good thing you're afraid to tell me, so out with it."

She didn't usually direct her patients like this; especially this adamantly. This was the kind of thing she was afraid would happen because of her emotional entwining with Rain's life. She knew she'd be squirming with unprofessional guilt later, but now she was afraid she'd shove her down, put her foot on her chest and pull the words out with a pliers if she had to.

Rain sat up straight and took a deep breath... "I met someone."

"Like a guy; like a boyfriend?"

"Too soon. We just met… in a fast food line. We talked and he bought me lunch and dinner."

"I think that's wonderful. You didn't run; that's good. What do you think? How do you feel? I don't have to ask if you'll see him again; that's written all over your face."

"If he calls." Rain admitted.

"When he calls… be prepared to cut out your tongue if you have to, so you don't say 'no'."

Rain giggled. Saying 'yes' was another non-existant to rare happening for her.

"What's his name?"

"Dalton."

"Dalton…?"

Rain looked confused.

"Dalton who… his last name?"

"I don't know." *Why didn't she know?*

"What does he do for a living?"

"I don't know. We never talked about that."

"Not to worry; there's time."

"Dr. McMasters?"

"Yes?"

"What do you think is wrong with me?"

Echo sat quietly. *'I don't know'* would not suffice here, and even though she was getting closer to forming an opinion… she didn't know. She had to be careful… she would go with the same answer she had given herself, when she asked it, after the divorce.

"**That nameless thing,** that comes from the forbidden gardens of life, through which we unknowingly stroll. When we finally name it, you will have the key and no garden of life will ever be forbidden to you again."

"**That nameless thing.**" She pondered the words in her head silently for a long time; so long in fact that Echo decided she was closing the session with her unspoken words.

****

105

Echo fought, all night, the urge to call Carl, her boy-toy. A boy-toy, that in her weakened state, she could fall in love with. It was morning now and she'd set the phone back down for the 3rd time... and the last. She picked it up and dialed.

"Good morning my Lady. Did you sleep well last night?" His voice was light and welcoming.

"I did." She lied.

"I've been thinking about you a lot..." '*Was that true?*' she wondered.

"Have you?" she smiled. "You were on my mind this morning... any chance you might think about me in the shower and decide to wash my back?" *Had she really said that? She was a bold, presumptious, needy bitch after all.* She held her breath... hoping.

"There's magic in your voice and I am already fantasizing about that. Sip on a cup of coffee and I'll be there before you finish it."

It had been far too long since she'd felt this fuzzy, tingly feeling. No coffee though... brush the teeth, the hair; prepare!

Then they were face to face; he grabbed her by the robe and pulled her in for a tongue lashing kiss. Pulling the robe open he stared at her pert nipples as she watched the bulge in his pants grow and his manhood became more and more engorged.

He backed her into the bedroom, the kiss in tact, but his hands were busy ripping his clothes off. Naked he pushed her back on the bed and straddled her. Placing his hands in hers and tangling fingers, he pushed her arms back on the bed, over her head and resumed the kiss. He attacked her nipples biting them until she cried out in pain; then devouring them, flicking them with his tongue.

It was perfection and he knew it; that burst of pain was the perfect foreplay for those tits. He knew that the enhanced arousal had traveled from her breasts to her belly... to her thighs and her clit would be as hard as her nipples. If she was a sexually sensitive woman, it would even flow inside.

"What do you want me to do next?" he whispered, his voice husky, his eyes on fire. "I await your command, hungry to grant your every desire." As he spoke his fingers slid inside her.

"I want you to feed me your cock. Right now, this moment… my desire is for you."

"But you're so wet; so ready for me."

"I will be ready for you after too and you won't disappoint me."

"There **is** magic in the words of my woman… I was right."

He crawled up her body and slipped the tip of his need between her lips. She played, toyed, circled it and then pushed her lips along his shaft over and over again. "Aaugghh…" He leaned his hands on the wall above her head and began to thrust as deep as she could take him, over and over, grunting and growling deep in his thoat until his semen filled her mouth. Squirting again and again until the over flow dribbled down her chin. He wiped her chin with the corner of the sheet and kissed her.

Mesmerized, she watched as his cock grew to full size as quickly as it had softened when he came in her mouth. Not three minutes had passed and he was ready for her again. She knew she'd never waste her time with men her own age again.

"Now where is that warm wet pussy." He asked his voice raspy, sexy.

He was moving down her body, stopping for a quick nibble on her neck, a quick bite of her nipple, a tongue lashing in her naval.

He enjoyed a bit lengthier attack on the hard nodule hidden in the lips just in front of his destination.

She was wreathing and screaming and pushing against his face as she came gasping out the words "Hurry, fuck me now!"

He thrust hard and held it deep. "Aaahhhh…" he sighed. "This is where it belongs." He began to move, harder, faster.

"Deep!" she demanded. "Oh god yes! Like that!"

Then she was wrapping her legs around him; digging her heels into his ass, pushing him deep and holding him there. She came stroking his cock with her spasms; losing all control, he released his bursting semen inside her.

Chapter 16

THE MOON IS PEEKING THROUGH, at intervals, as the clouds pass by. Ember is waiting for him on his patio; the smell of cinnamin tea all around. He stands in the doorway looking at her and wondering how he ever got so lucky. He moved to sit in the chair across from her. She picked up his foot and taking off his shoes and socks she massaged his feet while he sipped his tea.

She is naked, he is fully dressed. When the tea is gone and the massage complete, he stands and very slowly undresses before her eyes... she is hypnotized by his slow almost soft flowing movements.

He's in her mouth, but it's not what he wants this time. He pulls her to her feet and kissing her he backs her inside. The atmosphere is warm, deep and tender at first, but escalating rapidly towards hot, wild passion. Whispering her name, Task takes them both to the pinnacle of pleasure and the sudden release of accumulated sexual tension left them quivering against each other.

She lay in his arms more content than she'd ever been. There bodies belonged together; no doubts there. They liked the same movies, they could talk for hours, they danced well together. Together, no matter what they were doing, was perfection. Was this love and did he feel it too? Task... Mr. Jentaske; the cowboy she loved.

******

Sage was raging; she wanted this man… he was the kind of man she should have found. She hated watching while her sister lived the life that was supposed to be hers, but she had to or she would never discover what he wanted that Ember was not giving him. When she knew what that was, he would be hers. She would make it so.

****

River and Blaze were high in the mountains today. They had driven up together, but at the truck they had gone their separate ways. They would meet at the truck at sunset.

Blaze finished lunch and lay back on the rock trying to decide… swim or not swim. She hated that initial shock to her body as it hit the cold water, but she loved the exhilarating feeling that followed and the relaxed, refreshing feeling that she always ended the swim with. The swim won.

She stood, stripped and dove in. It was shallow, but not that shallow. The water was so cold that it felt like icicles jabbing into her skin like a knife; with a slight gasp she inhaled a small amount of water. She came up sputtering. A few coughs later she was fine and enjoying the freedom of the swim.

She'd have to cut this swim a little short because it was so cold, but she wasn't ready yet She lay on her back and closed her eyes, letting the current take her slowly downstream.

Numbed by the cold water she barely felt the arm slip around her throat. Her hands flew to the arm trying to pull it away.

"Am I going to get raped?" she wondered.

She felt the strength of the body that was holding her close to him. "You've done amazingly well." The voice whispered, raspy with emotion. "Your work is done, you are precious, you are loved and now you will rest."

The pain lasted less than a split second, she felt the warm blood flow from her neck; hot in comparison to the cold water. She sputtered and it was over. He held her, he cried and he was gone.

****

River jumped onto the rock where her clothes lay. "Blaze... Blaze!" he called out. "That water is too damn cold for swimming. Where the hell are y...?" His words trailed off as he saw her floating down the river a few feet away. "Hey, you okay? Get the hell out of that water."

Then he thought he saw someone disappearing into the woods and his heart tightened. *"It may only have been a shadow or an animal."* He thought, *"but something is wrong."* He ran down the river's edge until he reached her; seeing blood he plunged into the water. Reaching her and pulling her to him, he saw her neck.

"No... Blaze no."

Then quckly he pulled her body to the side of the river and headed into the woods after the man he thought he saw. He looked until dusk and then went back to care for his sister's body. It was gone; the river had taken it back and it must be headed downstream.

It was fully dark when he reached the truck and headed to town to report the loss of his third sister. There was no doubt now that these were not coincidences. His sisters were being targeted, but why?

How was he going to tell Rain? Blaze was dead; killed in the same way and almost positively by the same man as Snaper and Havannah. He knew the scenario... investigate the crime sceene; check out the body, but of course, this time, the body would be somewhere on the river and all evidence washed away... not that it made any difference. The police never found anything and both the other murders remained unsolved. This one would be no different. That's the ugly truth that he would be telling his family; he was sure of it.

****

Josh set the root beer floats down on the table.

"How did you get those in here unseen?" Rain asked grinning.

"I have my ways." he smiled. "Do I sense a rainbow colored bubble in that demeanor of yours?"

"I am feeling a little better about life, yes."

"Well I hope I had some small part to play in that."

"Of course you did; you've been a wonderful friend." She didn't want him to know how small though. She had to give some of the credit to Blaze after the way she felt in the mountains, but most of it was Dalton. Of course, she may not have been strong enough not to run like hell without the help of Echo, Quake and Josh.

"What have you got for me tonight?" she added, hoping to change the subject.

"Forgiving. I know little to nothing about your history, but I know we all have things to forgive and if we don't, it often hinders our moving on with our lives or building stong happy lives."

"Of course I have people to forgive, but I think I've done that for the most part."

"Denial of unforgiveness is common; it's not a lie... we just think we've settled it in our heart... or we've blocked it, or buried it and sometimes we just don't realize it's there. '*That happens to everyone; it's no big deal*' is a common excuse to bypass forgiveness. Our memories are a vital and permanent part of our lives; even the bad ones. If we have dealt with the bad ones they lose their power to hurt us."

"But how do we deal with our bad memories? Should we be dredging them back up just to deal with them and forgive them?"

"How we deal with them is the variable. It will depend on the circumstances. Should we be dredging them up... yes, if they have not been dealt with. If we don't, they will re-appear when we are at our weakest or at some other hard to handle time. Then they become stronger and can hurt us even more."

"Is that my homework? Looking for my pain?"

"Heavens no... you're not ready for that. Besides, you're already looking. That's what we're doing here, and with your psychiatrist and even with Quake. All I'm saying is, if a bad memory comes up to attack you... deal with it. That's your counter-attack. Get help if you need to, but don't let it hurt you and slither away to hurt you again down the road."

****

Breeze could not decide... was she Wendy or was she Tinker Bell. There was nothing exciting about Wendy. She was an ordinary girl... and talk about a boring costume. Tinker Bell it was.

She rented a boat, she hired a Captain Hook, she prepared an island feast and this would just have to be a pre-Wendy story. How on earth would she work in the lost boys? She pondered. She was going to challenge him to the hilt and see how he played it out.

She sent him his Peter Pan costume and the date and time with directions to the boat.

When he arrived, the music was playing and Tinkerbell was dancing with the 3 lost boys. They were all in a circle holding hands and doing a sort of square-dance thing.

"What's going on here? What are you boys up to?" Peter asked, as he boarded the boat.

"Tinker Bell says she's going to be our mother since you have not found us one."

"Tink! You know better than that. You are not mother-fied."

"I can be. I can make them take a bath and eat their vegetables."

"Flying around their heads until they get dizzy and fall in the river is not making them take a bath."

The first boy reached over and grabbed a boob and said, "We don't need vegetables anyway; we have these."

Peter took his stick and wacked the boy's hand and said, "Get off the ship. You are banned from here. You will not be allowed back until I find a real mother for you." The boy huffed off. *The initial look of surprise faded and she giggled. Jessie was the perfect Peter Pan. She jumped back into the fairy tale.*

"I can to be a mother. I can teach them school things."

The second boy snuggled up to her and said, "Yes and I can be teachers pet or at least I can pet teacher." He began to rub her derriere'.

Again Peter took his stick and wacked the boy's hand. "Get out of here. You are expelled." And the second boy was gone.

"Now Tink, let's be sensible here. You are not mother material. I will find the boys a mother; I just need more time."

The third boy tripped and hurt his knee and went crying over to Tink. "A mother could make this all better." He said to Peter. Turning to Tinker Bell he said, "Show Peter Pan that you can be a mother to me."

"But how; how do I fix that?" she asked.

"Why you kiss it of course." The boy said.

And she did. "Is that better now?"

He pointed to his thigh. "I think it needs another kiss here."

She kissed his thigh and said, "Is that better now?"

He pointed to his bulging appendage and said, "I think it needs another kiss here."

She leaned in to kiss it and Peter pulled her away. This time his stick was aimed at a far more damaging spot, as boy number three scramble out of reach and off the boat.

"Oh Peter, now I have no one. I am lonely."

He put his arms around her and pulled her close, careful not to hurt her wings.

"Tinker Bell, I am here now and I will take care of you... I will be with you."

"Promise?" she asked, with tears in her eyes. "Even if the mermaids come?"

"No matter what; you know how I feel about you Tink."

She fluttered her wings and they lit up like the stars, flashing all the colors of the rainbow. He was about to kiss her when...

"Ha, ha, ha... I've got you now Peter Pan and I'm taking back my ship."

Peter turned to find Captain Hook only 5 feet away, sword drawn.

"Go Tink; get back out of the way." He said moving between her and the Captain. Suddenly she was flying and Jessie looked at her in unbelief. "What the...?" *'That woman thinks of everything.' He thought.*

"I'm escaping to safety." She grinned, as she was being pulled up and out of reach.

Jessie wanted to give her more attention, but the Captain had just took a swing at him with his sword. Peter had to get his sword out and fight. They bantered about 10 minutes before she came back down. Peter had looked up several times, but each look had cost him a good clip with the Captain's sword.

Tinker Bell turned the music off and the extreemly loud ticking of the clock drowned out everything. The Captain froze in his tracks… listening. Peter Pan poked at his belly barely missing.

"Do you hear that?" Captain Hook asked.

"I do." Said Peter Pan.

"It's the Crock, isn't it?" He cowered.

"I believe it is." Said Peter.

The Captain screamed and ran off the ship hoping to escape with his life.

Tinker Bell ran to Peter and jumped into his arms. As he swung her around she said, "You saved me Peter; you've saved me."

He carried her below deck, her wings still lit and flashing. He lay her on the bed, careful to spread her wings so as not to break them. He leaned over to kiss her and saw what he could not see before, due to the dim lighting. There were holes where her nipples poked through and he dove for them. Moments into his feast he pulled back. "Does that mean that little shit actually touched that nipple?"

She grinned and he began to spit. She giggled.

"Relax Peter. The boy was wearing gloves and I cleaned it with a baby wipe while I was flying around above you."

"You sure?"

She rolled to her side and pulled the baby wipes from the waist band in the back.

"You little vamp; why do you torture me?" And then growling, he dove for her nipple again. "I want you naked."

"Then make me naked."

He pulled her up and took off her wings, then proceeded to remove her entire costume and lay her back on the bed. He began to undress and she said, "You can't make love to me."

"Why not?"

"A fairy can't have sex without Pixy Dust."

"Why?"

"It's magic opens the treasure. You can't enter without the magic."

Exasperated and fascinated he asked, "Tink, please, where can I get Pixy Dust?"

"There's a bag of Pixy Dust on my wings."

With the blink of an eye he had retrieved the wings. "Now what?"

"Pour a little in your hand and throw it up so it falls down over my body."

He did and colorful flecks drifted down covering her.

"Lick them off." She said softly.

"Lick them off?"

"Yes."

"They're edible?" he asked, flabbergasted.

"No of course not, but I'll call a doctor when I'm done with you."

"You're teasing me."

"Eat me Peter." She said firmly.

He began with her lips and worked his way down. She was sweet to the palate for the dust was made of sugar. She pulled his head tight against her external pleasures and her body starts to shudder, her legs quiver then stiffen and the orgasm grips her entire being. Her juices cover his face.

He moved up and kissed her. "Tink, do you have any idea how much I love you? You are unique in every way and I am more amazed every time my eyes behold you."

"You don't love me Peter. You love fucking me."

"Peter loves fucking you, but Jessie loves you."

Her head was spinning, screaming, "*no... he'll run; there is no Happily Ever After.*"

"Show me how much Peter loves fucking me."

He rolled over on his back beside her, his erection reaching for the sky. He watched as she poured Pixy Dust into her hand and he said, "Peter doesn't need Pixy Dust to make love."

"Yes he does. If he tries to make love without Pixy Dust, it shrinks to the size of a 7 year olds."

"Oh my! Sprinkle away!"

She threw it high up in the air and waited for it to fall. Then she crawled between his knees and slipped her lips over the tip, tasting the pre-cum seepage mixed with sugar. A slight whimper slipped from her lips. She leaned over him and he placed his man toy between her breasts and thrust as she held him tight. She pulled back and grabbed his butt cheeks and sunk him deep inside her mouth, sucking harder and forcing him deeper; moving her lips up and down over the shaft. She felt a strong spasm between her thighs. Her need was growing.

She looked up at him and he locked on to her eyes and said, "You need me. I can see it in your eyes; they're dark with need."

Amazed, she stopped moving; how could he know her so well? She released him and he pulled her up to him. Spreading her thighs, her eyes were begging to feel him inside her. His answer was... yes.

******

When Rain arrived home, River was there waiting for her. He told her all about Blaze. He held her and whispered, "Death shall not prevail, for even in death, life and love remain." He released her; she went to bed. When all feelings and emotions are frozen, it seems the only solution.

******

Dalton called and she did struggle with her fear, but in spite of her sister's death and the fear she didn't understand, she needed to be with him.

They dined out. He'd gotten a room on the off chance that she would need him for more than dinner; it had been a hunch, a feeling... something.

They were casual during dinner. They talked of his work, her session with Josh. He hoped Josh was old and ugly. They considered the weather and the President, the food and the excellent service. They discussed a couple of movies, but it was dinner conversation more than a desire to see one.

"I got a room with a fireplace, if you'd like to go somewhere quiet and private to talk or…"

"Yes, I'd like that."

She mixed drinks while he made the fire and threw pillows down on the rug in front of it. He kicked off his shoes and took off his shirt and sat down to wait for her. She kicked off her shoes and joined him.

The only light was from the fire and she was hypnotized by the way it flickered in his eyes. He brushed the hair from her face and kissed her ever so gently.

They talked. She told him of her sister's recent death and that it was the 3rd sister. "Except for the location, they were almost exactly the same. He expressed his sorrow for her loss and his fear for her safety. Then his fingers unbuttoned her blouse as his lips followed them moving slowly, step by step, down between her breasts and then to each nipple. Then he paused to remove the rest of her clothes and his.

His fingers glide gently down her arm in a warm caress and on down along her hips. One hand moves to cup her breast and take it into his mouth.

"Aaahhh." She sighs softly. He unselfishly continues to give her pleasure.

Soon, her lips move towards his erection, but he pulls her back up to him and kisses her. He positions himself between her legs in a sitting position, spreads her legs on each side of him and pulls her hips so her tush is resting in his lap. The tip of his manhood is touching the entrance to heaven and he enters her slowly, very slowly, so that they can watch and enjoy the increase of pleasure centimeter by centimeter.

When he has entered her fully he begins to move slowly, increasing… faster, harder, deeper until he hears, "Yes… aahhh; I'm cuming, oh god, I'm cuming."

As the aftermath of orgasm slows, so does his movements. He wants more, obviously, or he would have cum with her, but right now it was her pleasure… her comfort that was important. She knew what he was doing, but she wanted him again, so she held him tight inside her, clutching around him.

"What was that? What are you doing in there… what are you doing to my…?"

"I want you again. I need you to cum with me."

He raised up and moved his feet back so that he was now full length on top of her. He kissed her temple, cheek, nose, lips and moved to her neck nibbling. Still inside her he began to move. His breaths became deeper, faster, more ragged. Their tongues battled inside her mouth. And then, just as he was cuming, he bit her chin. She garbled out a loud moan of complete pleasure as she stiffened, released and came with him… the power of it shaking them both. He held her. They slept.

Chapter 17

SESSION 6…SHE LOOKED AT ECHO as a tear rolled down her face. She had been alone for the last 5 days, trying to sort out her life, her sessions, Josh's God, Quake's Creator and tomorrow; her future… her tomorrow. She wanted to believe that Dalton was her salvation, but deep down she knew that if she didn't make herself right, she would eventually destroy him.

"Rain…?" Echo felt a deep concern that she was unable to discern.

"I struggle to live one day and I struggle not to die the next." Rain said in earnest. "What do I do? I need to find **that nameless thing** before I am destroyed or I destroy someone else."

"I don't want you to lose hope. You have been doing so well. You are making progress, even if you don't see it… I do; I promise."

Rain fidgeted and looked down at her hands wringing in her lap. "Blaze died."

"Oh my god child, I'm so sorry; what happened?"

"She was hiking in the mountains… swimming, River said, and she was killed just like Snaper and Havannah. Someone cut her throat."

"Would you like to postpo… no, of couse not; you've never been a quiter. Can I get you something? Tea maybe? A drink?"

"Tea would be good… with honey if you have it."

"Sage is still following Ember and Task. River says she's viciously angry when she comes back from watching them. He's afraid for Ember and I've never seen him afraid before."

Echo sat silently… she wanted her to go on without guidance. She didn't want to lead her and possibly take her off the track of what she needed to say. She wanted the story of Ember and Task; to hear the romance and the…, but it was not her concern and Rain did not go in that direction.

A smile snuck across Rain's face as she said, "Breeze was Tinker Bell this time. I get so wrapped up in River's tales about her that I feel like I'm up in a balcony somewhere, watching it myself. Her love was Peter Pan and he got jealous when the lost boys tried to move in on her."

"I don't remember that in the story."

"No, it was a slight alteration in the Wendy be our mother theme."

"Where was Wendy?"

"She wasn't in the story yet. Breeze would never want to share."

"Were there decorations this time?"

"They were on a ship… a boat really, and Peter Pan had to fight Captain Hook."

"A real person or pretend?"

"Breeze hired some lost boys and a Captain Hook. After they were all off the boat they…" She relayed the story in perfect detail.

Echo wondered if her face was as flushed with sexual tension as she felt it was. She asked if there was anything else Rain wanted to talk about today, just so she could set her mind on less erotic things.

"I had dinner with Dalton again. I told him about my sisters and how they died."

"That's a good sign. Sharing personal things in your life is an important step in a relationship. Good for you." She wondered if and when she'd be ready to include physical communication in her new relationship, but she didn't ask. *"Leading the witness."* She thought.

****

When Echo got home her phone was flashing; she had four messages from Carl. His timing was impeccable. The sexual tension from Rain's stories still lingered in her body. She called him back. Yes, come over… He'd bring dinner… She'd take a quick shower and slip into a night gown; no… panties and bra. Her 51 year old breasts could use a little uplift.

He knocked.

She opened the door.

Then, as if someone had pushed a fast forward button, he grabbed her, kissed her and bolts of sexual anticipation shot through her body. She responded to him with identical fire burning enthusiasm.

They were on the floor with hot wet kisses and dirty little words. She wanted to explore his body inch by inch, she wanted to lick that sexy little butt, she wanted to taste his pleasure and feel his need sliding in and out of her.

His hands moved swiftly with knowing expertise to the most erotic spots on her body. She came for him and immediately she pushed him back on the floor. Hovering over him her lips consumed his throbing cock. She groaned as she tasted the early seepage of his satisfaction. He rolled her over, keeping his cock imbedded in her mouth, so that he was on top; she was sucking, he was thrusting. As he came, he pulled back, spraying semen on her breasts. His hands massaged the silky liquid over them and leaning down, he devoured her nipples. She was wreathing beneath him; he reached down and his fingers, slipping between the wet lips, caressing the hard tiny appendage hidden there. She came for him again.

"That's it woman; cum over and over for me."

He raised up and spread her thighs with his knee. He pushed inside her, fucking hard; the passion rising to a frenzy again. Their flesh slapped together as he took her all the way to orgasm number three.

****

"Our creator has the power to communicate in any method He chooses." Quake began. "He can heal us in any method He chooses. Sometimes it's as simple as a hug or laughter. Both are healing methods." He reached over and touched her hand. She smiled.

"Sometimes we cling to old hurts and disappointments even though we should have let them go. It's our choice, but like Adam and Eve, we like to blame situations and other people for our problems. Sometimes our pain and problems come from the way we think; our attitudes. We still need to learn a lot about the mind, how we think, how we process."

He changed the subject completely for no apparent reason. "The next time you go out hiking, practice using your instincts with small things; do you need a jacket, do you have enough water, should I take the camera... as you arrive somewhere, stop and see if it feels right. Stop occasionally and see if your instincts say go on or change direction. Learn to follow your instincts in small things that have small consequences. You learn by trial and error. Once you master the little things, you can feel more secure following your instincts in bigger more important things."

Again he changed the subject... this Indian friend of hers; her boss, was filling her with his Native wisdom and she could only hope to comprehend it in bits and pieces.

"Life includes suffering; coping with suffering is what builds our strength. Peace is not the absence of conflict, but the ability to cope with conflict. In our struggles, we often think we've met our limit, but it's not so. No matter how heavy the load, there is no straw that can break our back unless we give up and let it. No matter what happens... there is hope."

Chapter 18

Rain was meeting Dalton at the theater. He was the only thing in her life that seemed normal. He was waiting there when she arrived. Tickets, popcorn, soda… and his arm snuggly around her; it was so normal, so real, she was afraid it wasn't. They laughed together, shared sarcastic comments. When a tear manifested, he'd brush it from her face and smiled at her teasingly. If she only realized how everything about her endeared her to him more.

The sun had been bright when they entered the theater, a down pour had occurred in the interim and there was still a light sprinkle. Their motel was in walking distance and the light chill of the rain drops did not deter them from ignoring the offers from the cab drivers. He held her hand firmly in his. They walked as leisurely as if it was a warm sunny spring day; stopping for kisses at every corner and tender glances inbetween.

They picked up wine and Chinese on the way and in their room, with a shiver, she dropped her coat and scurried into the bathroom. When she came out, the lights were out and two small candles were lit.

As he watched, she unbuttoned her blouse, dropped it on the floor and kicked off her shoes. By now she was in his arms and as he kisses her, he pushed her skirt to the floor.

He sat down on the bed and just looked at her. The beige lace push up bra did it's job well; he felt his manhood twitching, growing as he stared, captivated by the soft clevage and full round mounds the bra created. His mouth open with deep slow breaths, his eyes moved up to hers; they caressed her face… the beauty of her eyes, the strength of her cheek bones, the willingness of her lips.

As his eyes moved down, even her collar bone aroused him. He admired her bosom once again as his eyes moved by. He followed the curve of her waistline to her perfectly rounded hips; the matching beige lace panties accentuating her beauty.

Her facial features, her body, were not perfect and still, she was perfectly beautiful. He was entranced by her; she stepped forward and his hand rested at her waist. He looked into her eyes and her fingers moved from his temple along his jawline to his chin and she leaned in to kiss him.

The heat of her body was like blue-fire flames… she couldn't breathe; her nipples were throbing though they hadn't been touched by anything but his eyes. Her body was tensing as though in pre-climax and she trembled.

He released her bra and cupped her brests devouring them. Then his fingers slipped inside her panties sliding them to the floor. As she stepped out of them, his hand moved between her thighs. She gasped at his touch. His need stood out firm and tall between them.

"So wet; so ready… I love the way you want me." he whispered, as he lay back on the bed pulling her with him. He entered, he listened to her body language and to her moans, he watched her eyes and face holding back as long as possible. When he saw that her passion was full, that she was ready, he gave her his all. His tongue warmed her mouth, his thrusting became hard and deep… faster and faster. He felt her tense and release as he emptied himself, holding deep inside her with his final thrust.

He lay there on her, skin to skin, face to face covering her with butterfly kisses and sweet tender words. When she shuddered one last time in the aftermath, he kissed her closed eyelids and then her lips.

As the afterglow slowly disappated he lifted off and whispered, "Dinner?"

She nodded.

"It's cold." He said pulling it from the bag.

"That's why God created microwaves." She grinned.

He grabbed the containers and headed for the microwave. They discussed the movie over dinner. She was going to clean up, but he stopped her. "I will help you later… after dessert."

"We didn't pick up anything for dessert."

He put his finger to his mouth, "Sshhh…" He led her still naked body to the bed and lay her down. He pulled a small basket from the bedside table. "Me first." He said firmly.

He dipped the strawberries in warm chocolate setting one in her naval, one at the V and one between her lips saying, "Don't eat it." He poured a little more chocolate over the naval and the V and covered her in whip cream. He began to eat; they shared the strawberry between her lips and he kissed her with power. He moved slowly, licking and sucking her breasts until they became clean. She was feeling quite bubbly now.

Little nibbles and kisses covered her as he moved down and spent an eternity at her naval. She was squirming as she pushed against him. There was giggling and teasing and arousal beyond compare, as he moved to the strawberry that protected her secret place of pleasure. The strawberry, the chocolate, the licking, the sucking, the gasping and moaning as she pushed against his tongue; the orgasm sending her spinning blissfully into paradise. She didn't think it could be any more perfect until he entered her, carrying her with him into a lightning bolt orgasm that opened heaven. She added that beauty to all the other beauty this man had brought her.

He held her and they dozed, but he woke to the feel of warm chocolate covering his soft appendage and a great deal of excess running back over his balls. Still soft she covered him with her lips and began the magic she never knew she had. When it was standing proudly at attention, she replaced her lips with her fingers and moved back to the more tender toys. She sucked on them until every drop of chocolate was gone before moving back to her main target. Then he was squirming and groaning. The moment her mouth covered him he was pushing into her lips. He was ready… no more play time; she moved over him with zeal.

Her tongue, her lips, her passion, all working together to bring the fulness of pleasure to this man she loved. She did love him, didn't she? If this wasn't love, she didn't think she could bare the added pressure of a stonger feeling; her heart would explode.

****

Task walks into the bedroom; Ember was peeking out from under the comforter. He peeled off his shirt and sat on the edge of the bed to take his socks off. Then he crawled across the bed towards her slowly pulling the covers off, inch by inch, revealing her naked body. His hard cock was almost ripping through his jeans. He's not wearing underwear and her eyes are fixed on his manhood. He moved up so his throbbing cock was in front of her mouth; he doesn't speak. They let their minds... their knowing of each other communicate.

She stares at the bulge in his jeans; like a snake ready to strike. She nibbled at it right through his jeans. The smile and the twinkle in his eyes as she looked up at him made her shiver. She unziped his jeans; she had freed him and it slammed against her lips as it burst free. She teased the tip and then propped a pillow under her head. She took the tip back in her mouth... and then a little more and a little more until she had all she could take and he was free to do whatever he so desired. He moves his hips gently as he slides in and out of her lips.

But enough... they both wanted to feel his fulness between her thighs. He moved back as she lifted her hips to receive him. She was trembling as he moved closer teasing her with the tip. She could only whimper with the need of him. He moved slowly inching his way to full depth. Unable to express how good he felt she simply moaned.

She brought her legs up and wrapped them around him as he began to move faster. She moved with his rhythm. With increased intensity and a few dirty erotic demands... they came together.

"I am in earnest; I want to pamper you, serve you, worship you... you are my goddess." He panted as he lay next to her.

****

126

Breeze loved him; why did he have to be her fairy tale? Maybe if they'd met at the grocery store or something normal… maybe then she could believe they could survive. No, Fairy tale or not… no one survived. There were no happy endings on this earth and she needed to run before it broke her. She had to leave him behind and she had to do it now. He had no phone number for her, he didn't know where she lived. She never gave him her last name. She had always contacted him. She would just have to stay away from any place they had ever been.

Tonight she would go to a bar far far on the other side of town. It was her Snow White fairytale. The 7 dwarfs were already waiting for her at the cabin in the woods just outside of town. Her prince would be expected to follow her an hour after she left the bar. That gave her playtime with the dwarfs. Multiple lovers… a plan she had never dared before, but she needed the distraction.

His name was Rudy and he had passed all the criteria with flying colors. She finished her drink, gave him directions and left. It was a 30 minute drive, but it would be worth it.

The 7 dwarfs waited for her in costume and obviously had started drinking without her.

"Did you pick your names like I asked?"

They lined up before her and the 1st one said, "Nasty." Each one gave their name, "Snake." "Bushlicker." "Handy." "Poontang." "Cock Holster."

"Really? Why?"

"I'm gay. I like it in the ass. You didn't say we all had to like pussy."

Disgusted by his words, she simply said, "You're right; I'm not even sure if I… and your name?" she asked the last one.

"Squirt."

She had nearly an hour before Rudy would arrive and they began to move in on her; she began to panic.

"Wait; I need to know the plan; what each of you plan to do." *Was she stalling? Why? This is what she wanted… right?*

Cock Holster perked up, "Nasty is going to take me in the other room, so if you'll excuse us..." They disappeared into one of the three bedrooms and Breeze sighed, "Two down." *Why did she feel relieved?*

"I'm going to screw you regular with my 8 inch..." she cut him off.

"Enough!!"

"I'm going to eat..."

She yelled again, cutting him off. "Enough!!""

Holy crap! What had she gotten herself into? How could she have ever thought this is what she wanted. They were childish in their behavior and attitude... they were vulgar, but they were doing their best to stay in character as I had requested.

Handy stepped up poking a finger in her face and said, "I'm going to finger you till..." Her glaring eyes stopped him flat.

"I'm going with doggy style Snow White." Poontang laughed.

"When do we start?" Handy asked.

"Aahhh, you guys know this is a Fairy Tale right?" she asked, looking from one to another. "A game... a fantasy, and you just play a part."

"Yeah, like you said; you wanted to hire us to help you play out your sexual fantasy of Snow White. I'm hard, can we get this show on the road?"

They were right, they had not misunderstood, but now she had to convince them that they had. This is exactly the intention that she had had. She was determined to use them all to forget Jessie, but that was before she was facing the reality of it.

"Look guys, you've misunderstood. I wanted you here to set the mood and put me in the glass coffin, so that the prince could find me; not to have sex with all of you. How could you think I could do that and still be able to have sex with the prince, who is my real fantasy."

"I came here to have sex bitch."

"And I paid you to be here as my employee; that makes me your boss. If I demanded sex, I would expect it, but I didn't, so just take your money, put me in the coffin and leave... please."

She was holding her breath. *What if they decided to take her; rape her... make her have sex? She could never undo that. It would be eating away at her forever.* For the first time since she started her fairy tales... she was scared.

There was grumbling, grunting, talking and finally shrugging.

"Pay us."

She paid them.

"Where's the damn coffin?"

"In the yard. There's no cover, but it is glass, so I need help getting into it and getting situated."

They all headed out. Three of them were actually little people and the rest were just really short men; adults 5'2" or under. Some of them were really pissed, but the others didn't care one way or the other as long as they got paid.

She felt totally exhausted from the tension of fear and the relief of her grateful escape. When the little men drove away, she still had 15 minutes before her prince was due. She actually fell asleep, so when he kissed her she almost choked on the apple for real.

He helped her out of the coffin and kissed her... prince professional. They danced. He played his part well and then he proposed and then...

"I know you're wet for me and my big cock will slide easily into your depths."

She gasped at the realization of how much his words discusted her. In her mind, she could see their thighs slapping together and thought she was going to throw up.

"Are you ready for me baby... uh... Snow White?"

"No." *"How in the hell did this guy pass my tests and turn out like this?"* she wondered.

He grabbed her and kissed her. He was rough and awkward. "I'm going to make you moan."

"Oh my god this is crazy." She said pulling from his arms. "Does that crap really work on women; it's revolting... disgusting. You are repulsive. The cabin is yours until 11 am tomorrow. Have a great time."

She grabbed her purse and left everything else and ran for her truck, leaving him staring in simple minded confusion. She stopped at a bar near by, hiding her truck in the back just in case. She really needed a couple of drinks to relax. She was still dressed as Snow White.

She was finally calming, but could feel the eyes on her. Then she met a guy who seemed really nice; romantic and loving. Though there was no setting, he did the scenario flawlessly. But in his room, when he went to lay her down, she froze. She suddenly realized that it wasn't the man or the discusting behavior, it was Jessie that held her back. She loved him and he had spoiled the fairy tale for her with anyone else.

She made her apologies and explanations and took her leave. She felt sad and alone. She was afraid to contact Jessie and she was afraid not to.

****

Sage was about to leave the house. She had to get to the coffee shop before Ember left. She was going to have to get rid of Ember somehow, but how? After tonight she would figure it out, she would have a plan; and Ember would be out of the picture forever.

Her car sputtered to a stop. "Shit, shit... why now?" She got out and slammed the door and started walking. This was an empty area, a field between neighborhoods and there were no streetlights and there were no sidewalks and there was no moon. The stars gave minimal light as did the glow from the city lights, but she still had to be careful with her footing.

There was no way she could go through with her plans for tonight. It would be all she could do to find someplace open that might help her with her car. Her mind was spinning with thoughts of annoyance with the change of plans, anger that her car had broken down, frustration that her life had turned to shit and an empty sadness that she could not explain.

Then suddenly someone covered her mouth and pulled her back into the trees. She struggled, but she could feel the strength of his body and she knew it was pointless. He held her firmly against him, his hand firmly over her mouth.

"Your ability to help passed as a child, but I hoped it would return. It has not and now you cause apprehension with your menacing ways. You are plummeting into a self-made pit, overcast with disappointment and disaster. Before the emnity gets too deep... to great; it has to end." His voice was raspy with emotion.

The pain lasted less than a split second, she felt the warmth of her blood as it flowed from her neck; she coughed and it was over. He held her, he cried and he was gone.

Chapter 19

HER NOTES BEGAN... SESSION 7... Rain Hardecky; 34

"Dalton and I went to a movie."

"You're still seeing him then?"

"Yes."

"And...?"

She was fidgeting, but she had to spit it out. "We're having sex. We've been having sex all along. I've never... it's amazing. In my wildest dreams I could not have imagined how wonderful it is."

"It's alright that you didn't tell me, but it might help to know the reason."

"Lot's of reasons... talking about my sister's sex is easy, but talking about my own is... and it's so special and personal. I didn't want to spoil that. You know how people in the movies are superstitious and think if they tell someone they will jinx it? I thought about that too. I realize though, that if I'm to get better, I need to tell you everything. I finally really have something to get better for and I don't want to do anything that might hurt Dalton. I have to get better or I might die."

"Why do you say that?"

There was a silence, she looked away... she looked back at Echo and said, "Sage died."

Echo could not hide the loud gasp that escaped her lips.

"Rain no; I'm so sorry. Please tell me she did not die in the same way…"

"Yes…, she did."

Echo had thought in passing, at one time, that maybe it was Rain killing her sisters, but it wasn't possible. She wasn't strong enough… emotionally or physically. Now she was re-considering the possibility of River, but she had absolutely nothing factual to go on. She had nothing more than a hunch and not even a strong one at that. She was in no position to make waves until she had more; if she ever did have more to go on.

"There's nothing I can say, so I won't even try. Just know that if you need anything… any time. I'm going to give you my direct cell number. Don't be afraid to use it."

Rain simply nodded. She was quiet for a while and no one spoke. Echo knew that silence could be a good thing. After nearly half an hour Rain began, "Breeze stopped seeing Jessie. She tried to find a new fairy tale guy. River said it was awful. She did a Snow White thing and the seven dwarfs wanted to have sex with her too. She came close to freaking out he said, but she got rid of them and then the prince turned out to be a really tacky guy and she left him at the alter."

"What will she do next do you think?"

"On the way home she stopped at a bar and found a really great guy I guess, but River said, when it came time to put out she backed out again. He thinks its cause she's really hooked on Jessie,"

"If that's true, why did she break it off with him?"

"She gets scared. She has a *'there's no such thing as a happily ever after'* fettish."

"I see."

The silence set in again and did not break… then time was up.

******

She no longer needed sexual details from Rain to go home horny. Just the thought of Carl did that for her. There were no messages on the machine. That was a first in the last two weeks. Even if he didn't want her to call him back, he'd call to say 'good morning' or just say 'hi beautiful'.

She called him. "You've reached Carl. I can't come to the phone right now, but please leave a message." She left a 'warm hello' and a 'miss ya'.

She repeated the scenario again the next night, twice the next night and the next. She waited another three days and began the calls again; finally after two weeks, he picked up.

"I'm sorry. I shouldn't have left you hanging like that. We had a good run you and I, but I'm rethinking where my life is going and…"

"I get it; it's okay. I understand." She said. "I want you to be happy with your life and we did have a good run. I'm not sorry and I have no regrets."

"Echo, I… no regrets here either. I have to go."

Her hand was shaking as she put down the phone. She had considered the fack that it wouldn't last once she'd accepted that it was good between them, but then she thought that maybe, just maybe it might work. Her chest was caving in on her… even if it did end, she didn't think it would happen this soon… maybe when the wrinkles got worse and she got fat or something.

She hit the shower and sexed up to the hilt. She knew she was doing it to prove to herself that she still had it, and Carl didn't matter, but she didn't care… it had to be done.

She sat drinking a bit heavier than usual, but she wasn't buying, so that was a good thing.

She'd had three different hits and this one wasm't 32, but 46 was still 5 years younger. A small ego boost. He wasn't a knock out, but he wasn't ugly and he had a flat belly. He danced slightly above average and he was hanging in there.

"Come home with me pretty lady; I'd like to take care of you. You are trying to hide it, but you seem a little sad tonight."

"That might be nice." She said softly and a little slurred. "I'm ready to go if you are. I certainly don't need to drink a lot more." *"Holy shit! Why didn't you just say… let's go fuck."* She thought to herself.

"The sooner the better." He replied.

He put on a movie and they snuggled on the couch. He would stop and kiss her now and then. When the movie was over he said, "Let's go upstairs." *No romance here; let's just get to it.*

She went into the bathroom and he called in that there was a robe hanging there that she could put on.

She took the drink he handed her and sat down on the bed. He went into the bathroom and she slipped into bed. When he came out he peeked under the covers and said, "Someone is naked."

"Dah..." was her only thought.

He disrobed and got in bed.

There was kissing, but she avoided it when possible. There was licking and sucking, but her heart wasn't in it. He was average length, but extreemly large in girth and she wondered if that was a good thing or a bad thing.

They fucked, but her orgasm evaded her and this did not look promising. An hour later he snuggled up to her ass and leaned her over to enter from behind. She threw the covers back and ran for the bathroom, throwing up until even the dry heaves had stopped.

This had all been a terrible mistake that she would not be making again anytime soon. She had paid the price for her choice and it was over. She left with appologies that she was sick and hailed a cab.

A long hot shower and 3 douches later she fell into bed, turned on the TV and vowed that making her mind a vegetable with crappy movies was the perfect solution.

Chapter 20

"How have you been Rain?" Josh asked giving her a hug.

"I've been better. Four sister's have died in the last couple of years… all murdered in the same way. My brother is sure now that someone is targeting our family. I'm supposed to be afraid and I guess I am, but I don't feel as threatened as he does."

"You've lost another sister; I'm so sorry. Your brother may be right though. You need to use extra precautions. Don't go out alone or at least be where other people are around. Be alert to your surroundings… and maybe you could take advantage of angel protection."

"Angel protection?"

"At conception, even before birth, God assigns you a guardian angel just as Satan assigns you a familiar spirit. That guardian angel gives you protection, but you can ask God to surround you with angels. The bible says "set Your angels around me to protect and preserve me".

"I believe in a God and I'm starting to think all that stuff about Jesus could really have some validity, but… well, does that make it okay for me to ask god to help me like that?"

"Many people, who are not yet Christians, call out to God in times of great need; He hears the voice of those He's still waiting to adopt just as He hears the voice of His children. Sometimes He says 'no' just like He does with His children, but in this case… if you will accept His help, it will be there for you."

"Wow, could you…?"

"Tonight you will be the center of my prayers and we will pray together before we leave if you like."

"Thank you."

"Okay, let's get started… a little bible trivia. 3 is the number of completeness and a symbol of the trinity Godhead. 4 is the world number. The river in Eden divided into four heads and flowed out into the earth. 5 is the number of redemption. The Israelites were redeemed with five piecss of silver. 6 is the number of man; sin. 7 is the number of perfection; righteousness. 8 is the number of resurrection and of a new order. 9… the last of the digits… is the symbol of fulness or ending. It signifies judgment. Aaahhh…"

"Yes?"

"I can't remember 10 and 11. This is embarrassing."

"Don't be silly. You can't remember everything all the time. Isn't that called human limitation?" she grinned.

"Right. Moving on then… 12 is the number of government hence the 12 tribes of Isreal. 13 is the number of rebellian."

Rain choked on her tea and after he pounded on her back and she regained composure, he moved on to other things. "You know the trinity is God the Father, God the Son and God the Holy Spirit. The Father and the Son have clear parts, but sometimes the purpose of the Holy Spirit is a little more difficult to understand.

First the Holy Spirit produces the New Birth. All who come to Christ are born of the Spirit. He came to teach and comfort. He brings all things to your remembrrance; He will guide you into all truth… listen and hear the wee small voice."

"Why He? All the characteristics of the Holy Spirit are female."

"Wow; I don't know. It never crossed my mind. I'll work on it."

She yawned, wishing she could take it back. He noticed her trying to hide it and chuckled. "Me too; let's call it a night."

"I'm sorry Josh, I…"

"Don't be silly. Next week then?"

"Next week." Rain knew that both Josh and Quake were careful not to make her feel forced upon. When they felt she was overwhelmed, they cut it quickly and without pressure. They both wanted her in their faith, but Josh said, "I just feed you; digestion and revelation are up to God." Quake said, "I feed you; the choice to digest is yours and belief must come from within."

****

They had a closing rotation at the coffee shop; every 3 weeks Ember had to do it. "Tonights the night." She had told Task. "Can we go tomorrow night?" So here she was, the cleaning complete and the cash drawer logged; she sent her last co-worker home. She went in the back, got her jacket and purse and headed out to lock up. She locked the front up tight, turned the closed-sign on, set the alarm and went out the back into the alley. The back door was an automatic lock.

She was exhausted, wished she'd driven instead of taking the bus. She neared the street only half a block from the bus stop when the arms wrapped around her.

"Task..." she started to say, but was stopped by the hand over her mouth.

"Was he taking this too far or was it not Task?" she thought as fear began seeping in.

"You learned love and you brought it into the essence. But now you're in the way. The doors have to open and there can be no door stops to trip over. I'm sorry, but you will rest now."

The pain lasted less than a split second, she felt the warmth as her blood flowed from her neck; she thought of Task and how she would miss him and it was over. He held her, he cried and he was gone.

****

It hadn't been more than 6 weeks since Sage died, yet as River spoke, she only felt empty. Still, in some unexplained way, she also felt rejuvenated, as if a battery in one section of her life had been replaced and was working now. In the silence of her room, her mind moved from the death of one sister to another. She realized that as she lost each one; they left her with something good; something that made her feel just a little stronger. Except Sage… she replaced the battery that gave her life when she was born, but she had grown bitter, so what had she felt at her death? She wasn't sure.

Dalton was working late, so he met her at the restaurant. She had ordered for him as he had asked and a drink was served as he sat down.

Half way through the meal they lapsed into silence; a comfortable one. They were eating and a pause was normal. Then she stopped, looked up at him. Before he could sense it and look at her she blirted out… "My sister, Ember… she's dead."

His head bolted up as he looked at her. "What?"

"My sister Ember was killed 3 nights ago." She thought he looked more confused than sad for her.

"Had you mentioned her before?" He asked.

"I guess not. I think I only told you about the ones who had died before and then when Sage…"

"Why is she saying this? Why is she telling me she died? Why…?"

His thoughts were interrupted by the waitress.

He would check things out tomorrow… he was confused, but he wouldn't fail her. "Rain I'm so sorry. What can I do to make this easier for you?" He reached over and laid his hand over hers.

In their room he held her. He wanted her, but if she was in (choke…) mourning…; he could not impose on her grieving.

The lights were low and she lay snuggled into his neck. She wanted him to touch her; to make her feel something good. She wanted to be face to face. She pulled away and sat up facing him. Sitting Indian style she tugged on his arm, indicating she wanted him to do the same.

They faced each other in silence. She looked deep into his eyes as her finger floated over his brow and gently down his face along his jaw line. Her eyes following the finger, shadowing the path leading to his lips.

As their eyes came back together her finger slipped between his lips; he sucked gently. Removing her finger she replaced it with her tongue. They were melting into each other through their eyes; they never closed them, but for the occasional blink. His hands moved slowly down her body in gentle caresses. Her nipples hardened under his touch and an overpowering need shot through her body. She sucked in her breath, unable to breathe out; their eyes still locked together.

She grabed a hold of his shirt and falling backwards she pulls him on top of her. He raised over her slowly removing her clothes, but his eyes never left hers. Then he broke contact just long enough to get up and take his clothes off; he stood before her, his erection at half-mast.

He leaned over her and bringing her feet over his shoulders he buried his face the curls. Working his tongue round and round, back and forth, as he sliped his fingers in the wet cave that his manhood was so hungry for. Her hips thrust against him taking the fingers deep as his tongue maintains it's course. She cums, grabbing his arms, pulling him up to her... begging him to fill her with his eager need.

Spreading her legs, he thrusts for all he's worth as she calls out, "Yes, yes, harder."

He is obedient, but it takes all his restraint to wait for her. He changes position only slightly hoping to last longer, but the new position sent her into an instant orgasm with the fulness of pleasures bursting through her. The heat of her flaming pussy is more than he can stand and he calls out her name, releasing and filling her with his satisfaction; emptying himself with one final thrust and a grunt of pure pleasure.

He held her; she slept.

****

'What had she meant? Ember died?' His mind was spinning as he went to the coffee shop and asked for her.

"I'm sorry, she's not here."

"When will she be in?"

"Her brother called and said she passed away."

"Passed away... how... but...?"

"I'm sorry. I don't have any of the details; that's all I know."

"Her brother called to quit her job via... passed away? It seemed so extreme." His mind was spinning again.

****

She forced her attention back on the words Quake was speaking. She felt guilty letting her mind drift that way; it was rude.

"Bears have many qualities we can learn from. We've learned much already through studies. Even science is at work. For instance, the fur on a polar bear is the best example of solar heating. Though the polar bear appears white to us, it's skin and fur are actually colorless. There is no pigmentation in a polar bears fur, but when the sunlight hits it, it appears white. By nature, bears are very playful even when their hunting or fishing. Bears use telepathy to communicate. The Dolphins have a different system of communication, but even more interesting is that trees communicate from as far as 50 yards apart. For instance, if there is a bug that can hurt or destroy the tree, it sends a message to neighboring trees so that when the bug arrives, a bitter substance has already been secreted into its leaves to discourage that bug from getting on it. Honeybees do a special dance to tell the others when they have found food. The coyote has special qualities that help it to survive. We are not exactly sure if it's a sense of smell or a hunch or what it is, but when poison is put out to kill animals the coyote somehow knows not to eat it."

"Oh please don't stop. You must have more for tonight."

"I do; different subject... small doses of a variation of things tonight."

"Okay."

"The white man, caucasians say they worship one God and most of them think my people worship many... like trees and eagles and tobacco. We do not; we too worship one God. You call him God, Jehovah, Father... things like that. We say Creator, He Who Gives Life, the Great Mystery. Though we do not worship the trees and eagles, we recognize and accept them as gifts from God the Creator and know that He has put them here to help us. We respect all of the Creator's creation. We use different things to create an atmosphere, a mood that releases us; things like sage and tobacco… often a symbol of what we are trying to communicate with the Creator or trying to show him our appreciation. Want more?"

"Yes."

"You once asked about the Vision Quest. A vision quest is not about looking for a ghost or spirit or seeing the future. It's about seeking wisdom and understanding from the stillness within us. Some Christians go on retreats to be alone with God; it makes it easier to communicate with Him. A vision quest has some similiarties with that. There is much preparation for the vision quest and when you are ready, we will go into more detail and the reasons for each one. Your mind is filled; this is pleanty for you to absorb."

She turned her recorder off and with a hug they parted ways.

****

Nearly devastated by her Snow White fiasco, Breeze wasn't sure what to do. She knew that Jessie and only Jessie could carry her fairy tale. She knew now, that she was unable to respond to the touch of another. She still held the fear that the pain would be far surpassed if he left her in the future than by her leaving him now, but she could think of nothing else. She would have to go back to him or give up the fairy tales and wait for… wait for what? All she knew was the fairy tales.

Going back to Jessie would be easy, for even though he'd wonder and maybe even be upset at the length of time that has lapsed, but he didn't know she'd left him… he didn't know she'd tried to be with another. Would he know when he looked into her eyes; would he sense her guilt. She had to take the chance. She could not be without him.

She sent him his costume for Beauty and the Beast. She rented a small dining hall and set up a small ajoining room as the elegant bedroom. The décor of the hall was elegant, the chef was there preparing the dinner and the music was set to come on remotely from her purse. The ballroom gown was waiting behind the shower curtain in the bathroom.

She waited patiently at the bar with a familiar bar tender grinning at her. She didn't remember which fairy tale he'd served her with before, but he'd grinned in that same way.

He set her drink down and said, "This one's on me. Is there any chance there's more girls like you out there somewhere?"

"Why whatever do you mean sir?"

"I mean a girl who cares enough about her man to go to such extreems to please him."

He was feeding her a beautiful compliment and it was like a slap in the face. Her fairy tales had not been for the pleasure of the man, but to fill her own selfish needs, commitment free. It wasn't like that now with Jessie; all she wanted to do was please him, but what if they'd met at the grocery store and she had come to feel this way about him? Would she have ever thought to arouse him with fairy tales? Maybe, for she had always been entranced by them, but when she imagined the fairy tale part 2... all her endings were crap. Part 2, in her dreams, were agonizing pain and seperation tormenting her... leaving her with a knowing that in fairy tales or in real life, even the most perfect things ended in pain. Would she have been afraid to do the fairy tales; afraid that they would tirgger a horrible ending.

She said, "Thank you for the compliment and I am sure there are many girls out there who would do anything for the man they love. Our problem is, we're often not sure what it takes. We can live the fairy tale, but we don't know what we need to do to make him happy all the way to "Happily Ever After".

"Well if he ever dumps... nah, no man in his right mind would ever let you go."

She'd taken the compliment gracefully on the outside, but on the inside she was feeling wave after wave of condemnation. Then she heard, "Belle, sweet caring Belle. How is your father?"

He spun her around on the stool and encased her in his arms, and kissing her, all those waves calmed. Inside and out she was smooth as glass. He could never have seen her betrayal in her eyes...

because in his arms, there was no other part of the world in existence; there was no other space in time... only right now, this moment.

****

Belle knocked on the door, shaking more from fear than from the cold. The stories she'd heard about the terrible beast that lived in this castle, on this god forsaken mountain, covered in dead trees and thorns that was fogged over unceasingly. Would he tear her apart on site.

Her head was always full of the plot; she needed it in order to be who she was supposed to be. Still, in her anticipation, she had to fight to keep the smile, that kept tugging on the corners of her mouth, off her face.

She knocked again and the door opened. Before her stood a massive beast; like an animal with angry red eyes, a long snout and long sharp teeth. He had claws like she'd never seen and he was covered in fur, but over the fur he was wearing a suit and tie of elegant and tasteful sytle. She gasped at the sight of him and took a step back.

"What do you want?!?!?" he yelled or growled or something.

She took another step back and her whole body shook with fear.

"My father is missing and I have reason to believe he may be imprisoned here. I've come to ask for mercy; that you will set him free."

"He was trespassing; a begger and why would I show him... or you, mercy? He came to steal from me."

He was harsh and angry, but she had to keep trying. "He was only lost, I'm sure. He was coming to ask directions and if he asked more than that from you, it was only because he'd been lost a long time and was hungry and cold."

"I will have to think on it. You'd best come in."

She hesitated, but what else could she do if she wanted to save her father.

"Your father is in the dungeon and food has been sent to him; you must be hungry too. Would you join me for dinner?"

"I'm not dinner, am I?"

He snickered at her attempt at humor. He could not stop the full blown grin as he thought, *"Yes, later and I can't wait to eat you."* But he said, "Not tonight. Dinner has already been prepared."

To her surprise the dinner conversation was remarkably pleasant... for a beast. In the end, it was agreed that if she stayed for the dancing, her father would be sent home, snug in a carraige. After hugs, her father left wrapped warm and with extra supplies in case the trip was delayed for any reason.

"He's not such a terrible beast after all." She thought.

"I shall go to freshen up before dancing." He said. "The primping room for ladies it right over there." He pointed.

She freshened and changed into the ball gown that was there and of which the beast was quite unaware.

He had his back to her when she entered the room and turned as she came close. There was no doubting, his reaction was of overwhelming appreciation for the way the dress emphasized her figure and her primping articulated her beauty.

She pressed the button in her purse and the music began... a waltz. It was bright and cheery and a bit faster than the usual. He reached for her hand and they danced... they talked over wine... they danced... they talked under the stars in the chill of the night... they danced; doing it all over and over again.

They were dancing and when he whispered, "I wish to take you my pet, for I am thirsty. I wish to drink your sweet wine; that which preceeds the taste of your passion." She melted, she could wait no longer.

"Take me Beast; I am ready."

He scooped her up and carried her to the bedroom. Lying on the bed she watched him as he removed the suit, but only the human suit. He remained in the costume of the beast. He came to her and tore the gown from her body; to find there was nothing beneath it. He put his chest out, beating it and growling.

Tearing the pants of the costume off, he threw himself at her, grabbing her hands and pinning them above her head. Spreading her thighs he thrust with the power of the beast. The sensations burst through her body; every nerve screaming 'fuck me'. Thrashing and slamming together, their bodies demanding as the vibrations of rising tensions escalated in a shared orgasm that would shame the gods; her pussy quivering around his waning cock as their sweaty bodies panted against each other.

"Oh my god; that was the hottest thing ever." She gasped.

"I thought my cock was going to burn and turn to ashes in there."

There was laughing and even giggling. Then showering, as the water refreshed them and their sensual prowes was reloaded.

The laughter subsided and the love making began; more gentle, less intense and then… the heat, the little bolts of pleasure shooting to all the perfect places of their bodies. There was love that penetrated between them in their eyes. Again their flesh was burning as wave after wave of orgasms cascaded through her body before he groaned the release that filled her with his essence… his semen… his fulness of satisfaction.

They slept.

****

Morning came to find him pushing gently at her derriere' with his early morning hard-on, while his finger sought the place of temptation in the curls. She squirmed back against him half asleep, but he'd found his target and the other half of sleep was quickly fading. She let him slip in the now wet cave. Once firmly imbedded there, he grabbed her ass and set them upright; she on her hands and knees and he behind her. In this position, he knew the exact angle to hit the target that would bring her to orgasm after orgasm. He played and teased her, moving on and off target until she turned to look at him, anger in her eyes.

"Beast." She said sweetly, though firmly and sarcastically.

"Yes, my dearest Belle."

"If you don't make me cum in the next 30 seconds, I'm going to rip your balls off with your own claws." She threw his costume at him.

"Then I will give you the best of the beast in me." he grinned.

In seconds she was screaming three consecutive orgasms; her body trembling and weak, her limbs quivering as he announced his own victory. He felt her weakness and let her crash down on the bed, but he held her hips tight so he remained within her; his body on hers was trembling too. He bit her neck softly and whispered...

Chapter 21

ECHO WOKE; THE DREAM AGAIN. She hadn't had that dream in 15 years; why was it back. It was the reason she became a psychiatrist in the first place. Her sister had been raped multiple times by 3 men, in every possible way imaginable. She was 17 and after being in a phsyc ward for 18 months, out patient therapy twice a week for 7 months, she stole a gun. She bought ammunition, hand cuffs and chains. She went to the bar that they had taken her from. She went every night, I suppose, until they showed up there.

When they piled in their car to leave, she jumped in the back seat gun in hand. She demanded the guy in the back get in the front. They drove to the lake where she had gotten a cabin. It was winter; litterly no one was there in the winter. She even had to find the owner in town to get the place.

At one time there would have been ice fishermen, but there had been a bad freeze and all the fish died about 4 years before. The restocking was yet to reach the desired level.

She took them inside where she had rigged iron bars. The bars could not be broken or pulled from where they were lodged without ripping out the whole wall. She had used what ever worked, so that the pipes were double sealed securely together. She had the first man, Bert, lock Taylan and Harold… arms around the pipe and hand cuffed. Then he put the chain around their waist and chained that to the pipe. The same with both feet.

She stood behind Bert and demanded he sit. She proceeded to secure him the same way.

"Damn it Janika; why are you doing this? All we did was fuck you a little. We ain't the first."

Her mental state had made it impossible for her testimony to be considered reliable. They had walked. Now they were all begging and trying to talk her out of this, but not a word had entered her mind. She had heard them, but nothing registered as discernable.

She aimed the gun at Harold's head. The other two kept talking, begging, being sorry... it was all registering now. She taped their mouths.

She cut their clothes off with a knife and watched them for 12 hours, getting colder and colder, while she sat well bundled. She didn't want them to die yet. She wanted to watch them suffer. She started a fire and kept it just warm enough to be sure they didn't go numb or sleep. Then she brought out food; every desireable thing she could think of... but not for them. She wasn't going to starve them either; she had other plans for how they would die, but they watched her eat for 36 hours before she fed them her garbage.

When she needed to sleep, she tied bells on each of them... everywhere; for the next 12 hours she dozed off and on. At the slightest move the bells would ring. She was taking no chances.

Now she felt rested enough to enjoy her next step, but the smell was getting bad. She had made them sit in their own urine and shit. She took buckets of cold water, throwing it over them; washing the worst of it away. Then spraying fragrance in the air, she began the next step.

She had read somewhere that sometimes Indian women were the ones to punish the men; especially if it was a sexual offense. The punishment was severe and '*wonderfully delicious*'. She thought.

One at a time, so the other two could watch, she began. She took Bert's penis, placing splinters all around the head and jamed then in the skin up and down the shaft. The wood had been soaked in gasoline, she lit them, watching them burn until they were ashes. Then she moved to Harold and then Taylan.

She recorded their screams; she didn't video tape, but the sounds from the moment they entered the cabin were all on tape.

She waited 2 hours and then took piano wire and wrapping it around the head of the penis, she pulled with the help of tools until it popped right off.

She waited 2 hours and took off another inch and then another...

"Now." she said. "Now it's time to die. I sort of wanted to let you go and spend the rest of your life with your balls hangin', your need for sex flourishing and no dick to get it with."

Taylan was writhing and trying to scream through the tape she had put back on, after the initial screaming from each torture. Another was sobbing and crying uncontrolably. The third silent, probably in shock. All bleeding.

The most horrible way to die in Janika's thoughts was to drown. That would be her choice for one of them, but if she was wrong, she could hope that her other choices might be the most horrible.

On day four she brought in a large tub and filled it with water. She took the chains and pulling Harold's feet wide apart, moved the tub between his legs. She had 2 bags of rocks held together by a short rope, the perfect length, which she put around his neck. Dropping them in the tub, it pulled his face into the water. She watched him drown. Harold was dead.

Bert she would cut apart piece by piece until he died. Morning came and she set up wire cutters of every size and knifes she'd had professionally sharpened. Every 10 minutes... ears, nose, fingers, toes, the left ball... continueing until he was dead.

She covered the bottom half of Taylan's body with gasoline and lit it. When the flames were fading, she coverd the top of his body and lit him up again.

She had hardly noticed the smell of old blood, burning flesh and stinking men... all she smelled was freedom. Nothing smelled as rancid, foul, hideous and revolting as her hatred for these men... as sickening as the memory of what they did to her. She knew that when they had suffered and they were gone her hate would be gone too and with her hate gone, the memory could fade.

She watched until his screams faded. The flames had burned the chair and it had collapsed starting the floor on fire. There was shouting and pounding on the door.

Hunters… hunting out of season, but they were there just the same. When she didn't answer, they looked in the window and saw it all. They had smelled the smoke and had come to investigate.

She accepted the fact that she would be locked up again, but it didn't matter. She felt nothing, but freedom and peace.

Ambulances were called, police arrived, trials were held; the crazy Janika was now in a psychiatric hospital for the criminally insane. Would she ever get out? Only time would tell. Echo had heard the testimony and the tapes over and over and the nightmares of the faceless demon, she thought to be herself, was doing these heinous things. She'd had the dream over and over until she herself sought psychiatric therapy.

About 2 years into her therapy she started school to become a psychiatrist herself. She was sure there had to be better therapy; she would find it. She was a doctor before she finished her therapy and the dreams had stopped. Now they were back. Why?

There would be no time to meditate on it now. Rain's 8th session was today and she felt so far away from helping her that she'd doubled the length of her session. She would expand their range of subjects she would talk about. Sometimes she didn't even think Rain needed her; that nothing was really wrong with her life, but if she was there, a need of some kind existed.

******

"River is following me every where I go."

"Why? Do you know?"

"Because Ember was killed."

"Rain, you didn't think it was important to tell me that?"

"I am telling you."

"Obviously your brother is afraid you might be next. He wants to protect you."

"Why not protect Breeze instead?"

151

"From what you've told me, River is much closer to you than your sisters. It's only natural, if he can only be there for one of you, that it would be you."

"I suppose that makes sense, but it's not what I want. At least I have a gun."

It did make sense of course, but Echo was beginning to feel stronger that maybe River was the problem… was he killing his sisters?

"Why is it that it's always River who is contacted when something happens?"

"We all carry his number as emergency contact."

"Where was he when Ember died?"

"Home asleep. He always goes to bed about the same time I do."

"And when your other sisters died? Was he always home?"

"I don't remember; what does it matter? Why are you asking me this?"

"Curious mostly. It just seems strange that he…" She had nothing concreat and upsetting her patient was not the way to go. "How did you handle the news of Ember's death?"

"Sex."

"River told you of Ember's murder, so you had sex?"

"No, my sister was dead and I had sex because I needed to think of happier things."

"I see."

"Dr. McMasters, why don't I cry?"

"I'm not sure. Some people don't cry when they lose someone because they feel that once they cry… it's like admitting they are gone; they'd have to admit that and face it… but they can't, not until they're ready. It's a form of denial."

"Will I ever cry?"

"I hope so."

"I told Dalton about Ember; it was weird."

"Weird how?"

"It was like he didn't believe me."

"Had he and Ember met?"

"No."

"That is strange... or not; maybe you just read him wrong."

"Maybe." But she wasn't convinced.

"Do you want to hear the Breeze story? She got back with Jessie."

"Of course. I'm happy for her. So what was her fantasy this time?"

"Beauty and the Beast." She detailed it out for her in perfection, just as River had told her. Sometimes she wondered if he made some of it up, but it was good anyway and why would he?

****

Echo didn't want to go home to an empty apartment... to a phone that wasn't flashing a message from Carl. She didn't want to go home to a bed that was giving her nightmares again. She didn't want to, but what else was she going to do.

She passed a restaurant and stopped for dinner. She passed a bar and considered a drink, but the memory of the last time talked her out of it. She passed a theater and went to a movie, though she could never tell you what she saw or what it was about. She stopped for gas even though she had three quarters of a tank.

She closed the door and threw her coat, purse and keys on the couch. It caught her eye; the phone was flashing. It wouldn't be Carl, so why bother to check it... it might be Rain.

She pushed play... "Hey, Echo... it's me; the idiot boyfriend... or idiot ex-boyfriend I guess is how you think of me. I have no idea what I was thinking. I'm sorry. Can we talk? Please... can we talk?"

She sat, her mouth open, her heart pounding... dare she hope? She wanted to call him right now and beg him to come over; she wanted to, but she didn't. She listened to the message over and over. She waited till morning. She waited till she was sure he was at work. She was afraid to talk to him, but she'd leave a message.

...at the beep... "Hi, it's Echo. I'm sorry I didn't return your call yesterday. I got home rather late and didn't want to chance waking you up. I'm fine ex-boyfriend and you are forgiven; of course we can talk. I'm free after 6 pm most nights as long as I know ahead of time. Let me know."

The next day was her day off and the thought of sitting there waiting for the phone to ring was unbearable… she headed for Victoria's Secret. She'd never done this before, but she had to try it… good or bad.

She bought a green crotchless teddy with built in uplift, matching garter belt and black net stockings. She found in disbelief… matching green, 3 inch heels and paid far too much for them, but…

She had Jack and coke and her Colorado Bull Dogs still untouched, but just in case she picked up his favorite… Chinese; shrimp, fire chicken and Broccoli and beef. If he didn't call… it mattered not, but if he did and she was not prepared, she'd hate herself forever.

She carried in all her goodies, carefully not looking at the phone. If it wasn't flashing, she didn't want to know it… not yet. She put the food away and headed for the bedroom to rip the tags off her new seduction package and lay it out to put on… in case…

She hit the shower and covered herself in lotion, used only lipstick and mascara, checked her nails for roughness and threw on a robe. She headed for the kitchen, but the flashing light of the phone pulled her like a magnet. She hit play…

"I'm not giving you a chance to change your mind. I'm coming over. I'll be there at 6:30. I will show you how grateful I am that you're willing to see me."

"6:30…that's 45 minutes." She thought, suddenly panicked. She pulled the Chinese from the frig and set it next to the micro. She made sure everything was in the frig for drinks and she set glasses on the counter.

Dashing to the bedroom, she put on his favorite perfume, blow dried her hair and slipped in to the seduction kit. She covered it with her slightly ragged old lady robe. She didn't want him to know that she…; not until she heard what he had to say and that he really wanted to be with her. She had her pride if he wasn't coming back to her.

The doorbell rang and she nearly threw up. She hesitated before opening the door; she shouldn't seem too anxious. She stood half behind the door as she opened it.

He wasn't looking her in the eye as he stepped in, but when he did he whispered, "Can you ever forgive me? There's no excuse for treating you that way; I was scared and I don't know why… not really."

"Come in; I'll fix us a drink; you can talk. I will listen."

He sat, she mixed drinks. "I'm sorry I'm not dressed. I only got your message 30 minutes ago; barely time for a shower." She lied.

She sat, he fidgeted and then he took her hands in his. "It was a dream that I can't even remember, but after that dream, I started having doubts about us; thoughts that I needed to let you go."

"There must have been a reason."

"My friends like you. They have no problem with the age thing. I'm crazy about you, so I don't have a problem with the age thing either."

"I'm crazy about you too, but I sometimes think about the age thing. If not before… I wonder when I'm 60 and you're 40; will you still want me? You must at some level think about that too. For me it's nothing. If I had that 10 years with you it would be wonderful, but for you it's different."

"Why? That 10 years would be wonderful for me too."

"Yes, maybe, but then if we were to end it, you'd be 10 years older looking for the perfect younger woman and wonder if you'd waited too long."

"I don't care; I want that 10 years… I want 50 years with you."

"I'd be 100."

"I don't care."

"Your family?"

"I don't care. I want you back in my arms. Can you forgive me?"

"Are you wearing underwear?"

"What? No. Why?"

She stood and faced him. She locked his eyes to hers. "Are you in earnest? Do you really want me?"

"Yes." He said standing to his feet.

She opened her robe and let it slide down her arms to the floor.

The smile that crossed his previously pleading face could never be replaced. If he was hers even 1 year; it was worth it... 1 day, 1 hour.

He took her in his arms, the kiss devouring her as though he could pull her into him this way. He stood back and looked at her, he nibbled her neck and sucked each nipple thorugh the teddy. Then he was on his knees probing into the curls, finding the lips that hid her pleasure. His tongue slipped into the crivice as he pulled her hips thrusting her pelvis forward. She gasped as his tongue made contact. He worked his magic, she called his name in the midst of her orgasm.

He picked her up and carried her to the bed. He removed the straps on the teddy, revealing her breasts and the hard flaming nipples calling to him. As his lips slipped over them his manhood slipped inside her. Tensions rising, she pushed up against him as he pushed deeper into her... thrusting harder, faster as the moans and grunts grew louder and the orgasm burst free.

And there was Chinese... and then naked, he sat on the couch; his full erection aiming up, begging to be consumed. It was her sole purpose in life to accommodate. She climbed on his lap, straddling him. He took a breast in each hand as she lowered herself onto his hard penis; slowly letting out her breath as he made contact with the different areas that pleased her.

"Aaww, oohh, aaww god yes." He grunted.

"Uh-huh..."

A spasm tightened around his cock; they both felt it. Their need suddenly demanding, his hands moved to her waist as he helped to guide her ride. All that was left was the whimper as the orgasm consumed them only seconds apart.

Chapter 22

"Whats wrong with me River?" Rain asked sadly.

"You were broken Rain; you were broken when you were a little girl, but you're getting better."

"Why don't I feel like I'm getting better?"

"Look at you Rain; don't you see how your life has changed? You have begun to feel things again. You care about people outside of this little world. You are stronger when you have to face a contridiction; you have learned how to find peace when your turmoil strikes. Soon all these things will begin to flow together as your own."

"My own? Nothing in this life has ever been mine, so how do I…?"

"Nothing? Have you forgotten about Dalton?"

She softened and her whole demeanor changed. "No, not forgotten; just afraid to hope. It seems he's attracted to me, but attraction is not commitment. I love… it is love, isn't it River?"

"To the best I can judge with what I know of love; what I've seen… yes, you love him."

She threw her arms around him. "You are all that's kept me going all these years. Don't ever leave me."

"I'll be here as long as you need me."

****

Breeze was thinking Pocahontus and John Smith. She'd get a cabin at the lake and rent a canoe. The rest of the plan was simple and today she was doing a dry run. She tried on her costume and took out the canoe to be sure she could handle it. Back on shore she sat watching the sunset and the rainbow of colors that reflected off the water.

His arms slipped around her; his smell familiar. She turned to see who might be hugging her. Before she could see him, his hand went around her face and over her mouth.

"Don't be afraid." He whispered. "You have done well Pocahontus; you are a good teacher, but she can do it now. She's almost free." There was a slight quiver in his voice, but it too seemed familiar. "It's time for you to rest."

The pain lasted less than a split second, the blood flowed from her throat, she saw the red of the sunset as her blood seeped into the sand and it was over. He held her, he cried and he was gone.

****

With the news of her sister, Quake decided to take her to the Sweat Lodge. "There is a cleansing in the sweat lodge; a cleansing of body, soul and spirit. You will fast the night before; water only. You will meditate before you enter and in that meditaion you will draw from within you. All your burdens, sorrows and pains will be symbolically left in the basket at the door as you enter.

The heat and steam from the rocks will make you sweat cleansing your body. Some have trouble in the moist heat and will spend some of their time concentrating on just breathing nice and slow… easy; this too has a way of opening your mind. You will forget that you are struggling to breathe and your mind will absorb what the Creator has for you. To be replenished, we need to empty ourselves."

She fasted and she meditated and she dropped everything that came to mind in the basket. She also struggled to breathe. She closed her eyes and concentrated on her breathing in order not to embarrass herself by crawling out the door before the time was up. There was more than one time that she had to force herself not to crawl out that door, gasping for breath.

Quake watched her struggle and prayed for her. Then the ceremony was complete and she realized that she was breathing fine and wondered how long that had been so. She remained until she was the only one left, just sort of wallowing in her victory; even if she hadn't been aware of that victory until it was over.

She racked her brain trying to remember the thoughts that may have been there during that time. She came to the conclusion that she had been emptied; at least for that period of time, since she remembered nothing.

Yet when Quake asked her what message she received, she had an answer. "Just that if I could conquer the breathing problem and remain... I could conquer all."

****

"I'm being transferred at my job." Josh said. "This will be our last session."

"That saddens me for me, but is it a good thing for you? Are you happy to be going?" Rain asked sadly.

"I am. It will be a nice raise, a job I will like better and I will be closer to my extended family. I will miss our sessions though and I will keep you in my prayers."

"Thank you."

"I recommend that you find another to study with or at the very least get a bible and search on your own."

"I'm not comfortable, right now, thinking about another teacher, but I will buy a bible and it may take a while, but I will read it."

"I will leave my email for you and if you have any questions, please, email me and ask. God is moving in your life even if you don't see it."

"I will take your word for that. So what do you have for me tonight?"

"I think I will leave you with a few scriptures that might be pertinent to your life."

"Tape is on; let's get on with it."

"Number 1…Fear is false evidence appearing real… One does not go to hell for what he does, meaning sin; he goes for what he doesn't do, meaning accept Christ's forgiveness. You are not condemned by what you do, but by who you are; who your father is, meaning God or satan; and the inheritance He has to offer you. If your father is satan you inherit from him eternity in hell; if your Father is God you inherit from Him eternity in Heaven… "For I know the plans I have for you." says the Lord. "Plans to prosper you and not harm you, plans to give you hope and a future. Then you will call on me and come and pray to me and I will listen to you." …when you email me, I will send you one more scripture a week if you like."

"I would like. I do feel good about this God of yours."

"There is one more thing I would like to share with you… with all the loss in your life."

"Please do."

"Memorial… is not a word to remind us of a death. It is to remind us that someone has lived. We can rejoice in that and the gift of whatever part of them we cherished, that is what is left behind."

She threw her arms around him. "I'm going to miss you."

****

His tongue probed for entrance as her lips parted to welcome him. Tender words followed and his voice was husky with need, her loins tightend, her nipples perked and his eyes glowed with fire as he moved to enter her. Moving with purpose, he took her over into exploding pleasure and she lay quivering beneath him.

He lay beside her, his eyes roaming slowly over her body… she was the perfection of imperfection; a beauty unexplainable.

****

They dined and talked and decided to skip the movie. All they wanted to see was each other. They played a game of Chess that she barely understood and then...

She was near delirious as his mouth, his tongue... she writhed against him as she overflowed her pleasure, legs quivering. Still she ached for more. She whimpered with a hunger not yet fulfilled.

"Please," she begged. "I need..."

He growled his pleasure as he moved to be inside her.

"Oh god yes!"

Moving rhythmically, Dalton kissed her eyelids, his tongue sliding along her jaw line. Then he nibbled her chin, sending a near orgasmic jolt of pleasure through her body. Feeling her shivers of delight, he succumbed to his own escalationg need... harder... faster; the pressure building until they journied together in euphoric release.

Weak and shaking, he lowered slowly, covering her with his body. The feel of his warm damp skin against hers was somehow strangely comforting.

They lay talking of future things with words like... someday, in the spring, when we retire; she wondered what it meant. The word love had not yet flowed between them; commitment was never mentioned, but for her at least, it was felt.

They slept.

The clock said 03:00 am; unable to sleep she got up and made tea. Wrapping herself in the afghan she stepped out onto the terrace. The moon was almost non-existant, but the stars were bright and beautiful.

She should have told him, but she didn't want to; she hated talking about it.

Having to tell Dr. McMasters was enough, but if Dalton was going to be a part of her life, he had to know what was happening in it. She would tell him at breakfast.

Then he was there, behind her, taking the afghan. He flung it over his shoulders and slipping his arms around her, he wrapped them both in it. "What are you doing out here?" he asked.

"I couldn't sleep. I made some tea; can I get you some?"

"No, I have all I need right here in my arms."

She snuggled back against him. She could feel his manhood twitching against her skin like a snake slithering by. This, together with the lingering aroma of their recent lovemaking floating into her nostrils, was sending tingling sensations to her most erotic places.

His tongue, his teeth, the sucking sensation on her neck sent a spasm inside her between her thighs. She was burning out of control as she turned to face him. This wasn't up against the wall passion. He felt her need to be one, consumed by each other. He knew she needed his strength and he lifted her leg and was inside her in one quick graceful move. Clutching her derriere' in his hands he held her firm and moved inside her; the sounds of their desire joining together and filling the air. Sparks of unspeakable sensations started a fire that was burning out of control; the erupting orgasm vibrated through their bodies.

Her legs quivered so profusely he had to pick her up and carry her inside. He too was still shaking; so completely drained that nothing was left except the pure afterglow of perfection.

He sat on the couch holding her; silent, relaxed... content and happy. In time, he got up and brought back tea for them both. She leaned back against him and sipped. Then, without emotion, she said, "Breeze was killed."

There was silence... for a long time he said nothing. Then... "Rain, I'm sorry."

There was more silence... he was about to speak, but what could he say? The questions he'd ask might be upsetting, the comments he'd make may be the same; he would find another way or at least another time.

****

He followed Rain as she pulled up to a small office building and went inside. He parked around the corner, but where he could still see her car. When she left, he would go inside and see... See what? What was he looking for? He didn't know, but he knew he couldn't ask her, even if he didn't know why.

Chapter 23

"Today I just want you to start talking; if I have a question or comment I will interject."

"Okay, Quake took me to a Sweat Lodge; do you know what that is?"

"I've heard a little. It looks like those round yard ovens the Indians have and they heat rocks and pour water on them for steam. You go inside and meditate together and it's some sort of purification thing."

"You did a great generalization of it. Just realize it is a generalization and understand that it's much more than that."

"Point taken."

"Josh, the guy I was studying with about God; he's moving away. We had our last session this week."

"I'm sorry; I know you really enjoyed that."

"I did. I'll miss him, but we're going to keep in touch by email."

"That's good."

Again emotionless, she said, "Breeze is dead."

"No emotion… no sympathy." Echo thought. *"It's not right; what am I missing?"* "The same way?" she asked.

"Yes."

"Can you tell me about it… or is it too much right now?"

"She was at the lake preparing and rehearsing for the Pocahontus and John Smith fairy tale. She was sitting on the beach and her blood stained the sand."

Echo could not help but notice, that last statement made her sad.

Then they talked of little nothings and dug back again into the past a bit. Going on seemed furitless and time would soon be up anyway.

****

Dalton went inside. There were three offices; a dentist, a gynecologist and a psychiatrist. Which to try first?

"Was she pregnant?" he wondered. *"That might explain the strange emotional behaviour."*

"Good morning sir. May I help you?"

"Good morning. I'm looking for my wife; she had an appointment here this morning I think."

"Her name sir?"

"Rain... Rain Hardecky."

"I'm sorry sir; we don't have any patient by that name."

"Ember Hardecky?"

"No sir. No Hardecky at all."

"I must have gotten the address wrong. Thank you."

"If it's the dentist, who cares; that won't help me figure things out." He thought, as he went in to Dr. McMaster's office.

"Good morning sir. Can I help you?"

"I'm looking for my wife. I believe she had an appointment here this morning."

"Your wife's name sir?"

"Rain... Rain Hardecky."

"Yes, she did sir, but I'm afraid you just missed her."

"Could I speak with the doctor please. It's very important."

"I'll see; one moment."

"Dr. McMasters, there's a Mr. Hardecky out here. He says Rain is his wife and he wants very much to talk to you."

"Wife?? She never mentioned being married; quite the opposite."
"Please, send him in."

"Mr. Hardecky, you realize that I can't tell you anything about our sessions."

"I'm sure she never told you she was married and I have some concerns. If you can't help me, maybe I can help you. Do you know why she keeps telling me her sisters are dead, when she knows that I know that's impossible."

"What makes you so sure she didn't tell me she was married?"

"Because she's not; I'm not her husband, though I've given it serious thought. I'm her boyfriend."

"Then we shouldn't be talking at all. If you'll exc..."

"No! Why does she say Breeze and Ember are dead? Why not just say we won't be playing them anymore?"

"Playing them? Breeze and Ember are her sister's, who were recently murdered." *"Shit, why had she revealed that?"*

"Dr. McMasters, I met Breeze first. She mesmerized me with her fairy tale fantasies."

"Then you are Jessie?"

"I am Jessie Dalton Jentaske, yes."

"I'm confused." Echo said, totally lost as to what he was saying. "So am I."

"Please explain."

"When I saw Breeze in that coffee shop, I was surprised, but not as surprised as I was when I was told her name was Ember. I figured it was just one of her fantasies, so I played along and it was wonderful. This was such a different part for her and she played it well. I had the best of both worlds... fantasy, sex and unsurpassed love. Then when I met Rain, I wasn't sure if I should call her Breeze or Ember, but before I could screw it up, she said Rain. Just another part of a wonderful woman. Rain needed me and lavished me. They all did... and though I wondered why the game and how long before we pulled it all together, it didn't matter. I loved her and I was in for the long haul, if she'd have me."

"Let me get this right? You met Breeze and intorduced yourself as Jessie?"

"Yes."

"You met Ember and intorduced yourself as Task?"

"Yes."

"Why?"

"She changed her name, so I figured I would too… so that I would fit into the game; the Fairy Tale."

"And to Rain you are Dalton?"

"Yes."

"You are one man dating all three women, but you say that it's the same woman using all different names?"

"Yes."

"And using all different personalities… correct?"

"You think I'm crazy?" He paused. "No, you think she's crazy."

There was a long silence; Echo was processing.

"If what you say is true, then I think she may have multiple personalities… yes it's possible. Are you still in it for the long haul?"

"Yes, of course. I've always known she was one woman filled with the spice of life. I love her."

"I've studied this of course, but she would be my first, if it really is the case. Against all laws and better judgement… I'm bringing you into this, if you are willing to help."

"Anything." He said firmly.

"There were four other sisters… they all died the same way."

"Yes, she mentioned them." He acknowledged.

"Could they be her too?" She shook her head. "Or maybe it was their deaths that brought this on. I should try to get in touch with her brother." She was thinking outloud more than talking to him. "Dalton, I need some time to sort this out. Could you come back in day after tomorrow?"

"Whatever it takes."

"2 o'clock. And can you pretend you don't know all of this. Just until then. We don't want to traumatize her if we've got this wrong."

******

"Dalton, Rain is an only child. She has no sisters, nor does she have a brother. What I need from you is to just keep seeing her and not let her know we know anything. I have to research both her life and case histories. Can you give me a few more days? I'll work around the clock."

"Take all the time you need. Romancing my woman is not a problem. It's just that I can't keep decieving her. This needs to be out in the open. I'm just glad it makes sense now."

"What worries me is why they are all dieing now."

"I get it; never thought of that."

"I'll call you… as soon as possible." She assured him.

****

Dalton spent the next 24 hours processing; he fully understood what Echo was feeling; the difference was there was nothing he could do. 24 hours later he realized he was wrong. He'd thought about his three loves seperately and together. Breeze lived the freedom that Rain was afraid to experience, but even then she dared not permit or accept a promise of tomorrow. Ember was Rain… like her in nearly every way except for the sadness, a melancholy that he watched disappear in his arms. How could he not have known; how could he believe she could live these different lives and think it normal? Well, not normal; just eccentric… beautifully eccentric. She had been all that he needed; all that he'd ever imagined and more. Now it was his turn to be all that she needed.

He called work and took a months sabbatical; warning them that the time could double. Of course they gave him a hard time, but he told them it was a family emergency and it was not optional.

"Fire me if you have to." He said adamately.

"Dalton, you know better than that. I don't have a better man in the company and you've covered our ass more times than I can count. It won't be easy without you, but… Just get back when you can; we need you."

"Thanks Bob."

He hadn't had more than a one day vacation in 4 years. He had 90 days of Family Medical Emergency and 3 months of vacation coming and that didn't include the 5 months that he'd forfeited. He didn't like his boss, but he loved his job and the people he worked with. He didn't want to go elsewhere, but he knew he could if need be and so did Bob.

He called Rain and begged her for a "slumber party".

She giggled. "When?"

"Now, I'll pick you up in two hours. No, make it three; I have to hit the mall and the grocery. Don't pack a thing. Your overnight bag is here and I'll get everything else... even jammies are on me."

"Are you sure? I can..."

"All I want is you."

"I'll be ready."

She hit the shower and he headed for the mall. Two sets of baby doll pajamas, a night gown, two robes and slippers later he headed for the video store. 6 movies later he headed for the grocery store; it had to be perfect for her... and fun. There would be popcorn and floats and pizza and chips and BBQ's... and 6 flavors of icecream.

He picked her up with 7 minutes to spare. She looked at all the bags in the back and laughed. "Is it just us or are you having a slumber party for 10?"

"It's a double sleep over... two nights."

"Looks like you prepared for two weeks."

He grinned and leaned in for a kiss.

He wouldn't let her help haul stuff in, so she went into the living room and dropped down on the couch. The coffee table had been moved and there were piles of blanket and pillows spread all over the floor. *"He's really serioius about this."* She thought. She had never had or been to a slumber party herself, but had seen all the variations on TV. Non of which included a boy or a man.

He threw a bag at her and said, "Your jammies... go change."

She'd never seen silk baby dolls before. They were baby blue with matching slippers and a short robe. The robe she laid over the arm of the couch, kicked off the slippers and snuggled around a pillow on the floor.

Shortly he came in with pizza, chips and root beer floats. "Hungry?" he asked.

"I am, but I should be serving you."

"You spoil me all the time; it's my turn." He insisted, handing her the box of pizza.

He set the tray on the coffee table and leaned over and kissed her. "Which movie?" He asked handing her all six.

"Oh my, you did get some that you like and not just for me, right?"

"I didn't really think about that. I just tried to get all different kinds."

She looked through them... 'Titanic', 'Mind Hunters', 'Saw', 'Death, Demons and Desire', 'The Hungar Games' and 'Twilight'. He remembered that they'd seen the first two. She closed her eyes, shuffled them in a pile and picked one... Mind Hunters.

With dinner behind them and the movie half over they snuggled down on the pillows to finished the movie. Then out of know where, he was beating the crap out of her with a pillow.

"What the..." she screamed, jumping up and grabbing a pillow of her own and smacking him with it. Panting and laughing they collapsed on the floor.

He pulled her to him, burying his tongue between her lips as they thrashed around removing clothes, touching, feeling... entering. She pushed up, forcing him deeper. As she squirmed, each move caused a variety of sensations, bringing them quickly to a frenzy of uncontrolled passion. His forceful thrusting gaining momentum, she couldn't control the mournful sounding screams as she exploded in orgasm. He followed close behind.

They lay together with tender kisses and soft caresses. When he moved beside her, she felt like he had stripped her of her life.

"What's wrong?" he asked, deep concern in his voice.

"Nothing, everything is perfect; it's just that I feel so alive with you inside me. Sometimes it's like a shock to my body when you move away."

"I feel that too. I am not all that I am unless we are one." He kissed her. "But it was not my intention to move away too far. I only wanted to turn you over and ravish you in another style." He grinned. She grinned back, turning over.

"You must read my mind." She said, wiggling her ass in his face.

He kissed it, caressed her derriere' with his tongue and then eagerly thrust back inside her. She was euphoric with pleasure; wanting to sheathe his cock there and never let him go. Her whimpers and groans of pleasure were driving him crazy. Then he too, was out of control. He grabed her behind and holding it tight, speaking and grunting deep throaty words of need, he thrusts into her deep and hard over and over until... she felt his warm injection bringing her to the full release of her own pleasure.

He rolled off and pulled her into his arms. "You are too much woman; you make me happy."

She was sure she'd never made anyone happy before, but she said with earnest, "Not possibly as happy as you make me."

He kissed her tenderly and then jumped up and said, "Popcorn, cookies or ice cream? ...or all of the above?"

"Ice cream, but you have to let me help you."

He reached down and taking her hand he pulled her up, smashing her boobs against his chest. "You just did." He teased.

He was very diligently scooping away at the very frozen ice cream when she slipped her arms around his waist and cupped his special purpose in her hands.

"What are you doing?" he grinned.

"I'm helping."

"Helping what?"

"Helping myself."

"Indeed you are."

He turned to face her and dropped the scoop of ice cream on her breast. Then he pulled her tight against him, smashing it. When he leaned down to lick it off her breast, she asked, "What are you doing?"

"Helping myself. It's a really good idea you had there."

She giggled and pulled away. "Don't tease me; I'm hungry."

He filled the bowls and they put on The Hungar Games.

******

They slept late and when she woke it was to the smell of bacon. He was making her breakfast. He brought her coffee to her in bed.

"Three tablespoons creamer and two packs of stivia... yes?"

"Perfect, but I should be getting you coffee."

"You have... over and over."

"Thank you." She whispered.

"Breakfast will be ready in 15 minutes. We'll eat in the living room and watch another movie."

She rinsed off in the shower and put on the nightgown he had bought her. When she walked into the living room he was setting the tray on the coffee table.

He sat down, still naked, with his limp appendage in his lap. She didn't even kiss him. She went straight for his lap and... she was working her magic; the magic she didn't know she had until Dalton. She worked until he had a perfect hard-on. Then... she threw her leg across his lap and straddling him, she wrapped the engorged member deep inside her... wet and warm. He guided her with his hands; rocking her crevice around his need. He pushed up into her and she began to shudder as the orgasm gushed thrugh her and the spasms sent him into his own world of orgasm.

Restarting the movie, he warmed breadfast... that's why God created microwaves.

Chapter 24

Echo called Dalton.

"This appears to be far more complicated than we thought. What it looks like is not just multiple personalities, but I think it's complicated with schizophrenia. I think she's had delusions and hallucinations both visual and auditory. Visual hallucinations are far more rare and not usually found with schizophrenia. I think everything she's told me are her own experiences; she's just having them under the identity of her sisters. This could be difficult and lengthy; are you still in?"

"All the way."

"Please be sure, because if we get in there with her and you bolt, it could set her back or worse; create new personalities and hallucinations."

"I'm in... all the way; for the long hall... no matter what."

"Can you come for her session this afternoon?"

"I've taken the next month off; more if I need it. I'm all hers and yours... what ever you need me to do." He assured her.

****

"Rain, I think we've found what it is that has you so confused and insecure. I've canceled all my clients for today, so we have all the time we need to talk about it. Dalton will be joining us, if that's alright with you."

"Dalton?" Panic gripped her as she fought falling into a comatose state. "How does he even know I'm here; that I'm in therapy."

"I think he should explain; if you'll let him."

"He'll hate me. He'll think I'm crazy or dangerous. He won't want to be with me now. Why did you tell him? That's wrong."

"She didn't tell me." he said, coming into the room. "I told her. It bothered me, what you told me about Ember and Breeze, so I followed you here. I'm sorry. I was worried about you."

"I understand" Rain said; her head dropping down, afraid to look at him. "You can leave now. It's not your fault I'm like this. I... you..."

"I'm not going anywhere. I love you; I want to help you and I'm going to stay with you through this. Then we can start our life together, free and clear."

"You... love me?" She looked at him in disbelief.

"I love you."

"Free and clear of what?" she asked, afraid of the answer. "And why did Breeze and Ember's death bother you and not the others."

"Your demons; not real demons... your problems, the ones that hinder your freedom. You can be free of them."

Freedom? That's what River always says. She thought. "I don't understand." She said, shaking her head.

He sat next to her and put his arm around her. "I'll let Echo... Dr. McMasters take it from here."

"Rain, I have a theory; one I believe is the truth... reality. It's going to be very difficult for you to hear and to accept, but until you do... you will not heal. Are you willing to listen and consider the possibility of what I say before rejecting it completely?"

She looked at Dalton. "Do you agree with her?"

"I think she might be right, yes."

She looked back at Echo; fear clutching at her, twisting her insides and still she said, "Alright... yes, I'll listen."

"I believe you have multiple personalities. Maybe, because of recent events, that maybe, some of them are gone now."

"You mean like I have different people inside me with different personalities? They think my body is there's, but none of us know each other? I've seen that on TV, but…"

"That's a very interesting way of putting it, but yes… that's almost exactly what I mean."

"Who are they? Why do you think they are gone?"

"Blaze maybe, but most certainly, Ember, Breeze and…"

"My sisters, but that's impossible. Besides they have died."

"Yes… exactly. And when they died, those personalities stopped appearing; stopped presenting themselves in your body or in your mind."

"What makes you think that? What makes you think my sisters live inside me?"

"Me." Dalton said.

Her head spun around to face him. "You? But…"

"Rain, I met Breeze first, before you." Dalton said.

"What do you mean?"

"My name is Jessie Dalton Jentaske. I met Breeze and gave her the name Jessie. She… you didn't want my last name; not at first."

"But…"

"Let me finish."

She nodded.

"Then I went in that coffee shop and saw you there, but you said your name was Ember. I thought it was part of your fantasy game. Breeze's fantasy game, so I gave my last name… Task; short for Jentaske. Rain, both Breeze and Ember were you."

"How… if I were Breeze and you met me as Ember, why wouldn't I know you were Jessie?"

"Because your personalities rarely knew what the other was doing." Echo interjected. "They never met each other's boyfriend."

"Then when I met you," Dalton went on, "you gave me the name Rain. I wanted to play the game to please you; the Breeze you. So I gave you my middle name… Dalton."

"Why… why would I do that? I'd have to create them wouldn't I?"

"Yes, as to why I can only speculate." Echo paused as Rain changed her focus from Dalton to her.

"But I saw my sisters, I talked to them. I couldn't do that if I **was** them."

"It's more complicated than that. It appears that you also have hallucinations; delusions."

"But why? Why would I immagine my sisters?"

"Like I said, I can only speculate. Your childhood was less than desireable and it left you with needs. You may have created your sisters to fill those needs. Needs that you were to afraid to fulfill yourself. If you created them, you could do those things and not be responsible; if they failed or made mistakes, they would not be yours."

"And Blaze?"

"Yesterday when I called you in for an unscheduled session and we talked about your more extended family; I think you revealed a lot... again, for now, it's speculation, but let's begin with that."

"Alright."

"You told me about your mother's sister who was never allowed to come in the house, so she came by when your dad was away and you visited in the yard. You said she was loving and soft spoken and happy; that she was the only one you ever remembered hugging you or your mom. She talked about her marriage and it sounded like the fairy tales you loved so much as a child. She talked about God and you always wished you could see her more, but she died when you were around 11. I think you created Ember to be like her."

"She was sort of like her, wasn't she? I never thought about it." Rain said softly, almost speaking to herself.

"Then you told me about over hearing your father and his brother Henry talking and laughing about sex. When you hit puberty you paid more attention and became curious, but your mother had suffered so much from it that you were afraid. In some way you must have bleneded their filth talk and your normal curiosity with your fairy tales... thus you got Breeze."

"Breeze's stories were rather kinky at first, but they became more beautiful after she met Jessie." She looked at Dalton and swallowed hard. She couldn't comprehend it; those stories were hers? Dalton slept with her sister? But he thought it was me? It's all too... too... Her head was spinning.

"The seven of you, being one will take a little time to sort out. The 3 of you, being one with Dalton will also take a little time to sort out, but look at it this way; you both know each other better as three than you did individually."

Dalton and Rain looked at each other thinking... *"Does she really think that makes it easier to swallow?"*

"Okay, so maybe that wasn't a light bulb idea." Echo said. "This is new to me too. If you want to bring in another psychiatrist..."

"No, just you." Rain insisted.

They all looked at each other and began laughing... hard. They didn't know if it was funny or if the tension required this relief or if they had all just lost it, but it felt good.

"There's just one more thing and then I want you to go and process this together for a couple of days before we go on."

"Sure." They said together. Neither was sure they could handle any more.

"You also told me about your mother's sister's daughter... your cousin. She was 12 or 13 to your 9 or 10. She would come over sometimes and take you to the foothills on the edge of town. You'd climb around and watch the clouds and chase rabbits; things like that. You said it always made you peaceful cause you didn't think about home. She told you it was the peace of God, but you didn't know if that was true."

"Yes, I remember."

"I think that's where Blaze came from."

There was silence, closing comments and departure.

Echo and Rain hugged for the first time; at least that she could remember.

Dalton took her back home with him.

Chapter 25

FOR DALTON, THE SILENCE WAS deafening as Rain's mind was spinning out of control. He could feel the chaos bouncing inside her head just watching her face. He wanted to comfort her, but he had no idea what to say and he was afraid he'd spook her if he tried. He held her hand all the way home; bodily contact was all he had to offer her.

He didn't want to leave her, but he could feel her tension rising and felt her need to be alone, so he went to return the video's they had watched. When he returned, she met him at the door in the flowing black gown that he had bought her. She handed him a glass of wine and delivered a light kiss. As he followed her to the candle lit table and sat across from her, he wondered if she was escaping into another personality. She'd prepared a light dinner, one of his favorites. There was no conversation except with their eyes.

She poured them a second glass of wine. He took her by the hand and led her to the fire. They stood floating in each other's eyes. If this was another personality, he would love her too; she was perfection whatever name she used.

He kissed her, slow and lingering and as his hands glide to her waist, hips... tush, he realizes she has nothing on underneath. He drops to his knees and slides the gown up burying his face in the V. She selfishly takes the pleasures he offers. But tonight, her pleasure is his pleasure above all else. She guides him to his feet and slides his shirt off his shoulders, turning each tiny nipple into a little rock between her teeth.

Unzipping his jeans she feels his hardness pushing to be free. She kneels and taking him to her lips she begins… slowly, gently licking, sucking, playing… enjoying his pleasure.

He stops her, pulling her up to him; kissing her deeply.

She led him to the hot tub. He was watching her let her gown drop, inch by inch over her shoulders, her breasts, her naval, her hips and to the floor, his eyes following every inch. She slips into the water and reaches for him to follow. They made love, sweet, gentle, tender. He bathed her in the most beautiful words and whispering her name, he kissed her.

He felt her tense slightly. What had he done wrong? He would make what ever it was up to her. He began to nibble her neck. She moaned and the light bulb came on. Was she afraid of her other names? Has this knowledge made her more insecure? He would be careful… she was Rain.

He began sucking her neck again. The desire, the passion sky-rocketed in leaps and bounds as they begin making those wonder-ful, familiar sounds; he moves faster, harder, as the water splashes and their wet flesh slaps loudly against each other and they cum… "Aaahh… oh god yesss."

He collapses over her and they slide down into the welcoming water. "This is only the beginning." He whispers. *They had success-fully deleted every thought, that Echo had put there, from their minds… for now.*

The heat was overcoming them; it was time to get out. The eve-ning sprinklers came on as they headed for the house. It was refresh-ing and welcome.

****

Session 12… Dalton and Rain sat across from Echo holding hands.

"Are you ready to begin." She asked.

They nodded.

"I'd like to stay today until we examine your other sisters, if that's alright with you."

"I insist; I want this over. Were they real or other personalities living in me?"

"The public records of your family show you are an only child."

"Except my brother; I'm the only girl."

"We'll get into all that later if that's okay. One step at a time."

Rain felt a fear she didn't understand, but her doctor knew best how to do this… she was sure; wasn't she?

"Let's go back to the extended family information. Your mother's sister talked a lot about God. Ember came from her ability to love and I believe Havannah came to help you dig deeper into God, so you could investigate those beliefs further; opening a door for another way for you to find answers. You wanted to know if there was any substance to your Aunt's beliefs."

"I'm crazy… not just sick. I'm…"

"Hurting; needing comfort and understanding. That's not sick. It's a normal need and you found that in the only way you could. It's not the same as… May we just move on?"

"Please, how much worse can it get?" she sighed.

"Please understand that this is all new information. I'm only walking on intuition and an educated guess. I have to research a lot after each session, but it's where we have to start. We have a long, long way to go. Are you ready to move on?" Echo asked.

"I guess." She said with a sigh. Dalton pulled her tighter.

"You had a cousin on your dad's side of the family. She rode a motorcycle, she was stubborn and strong willed. She never backed down, even if she knew she was wrong. You admired her strength and you may have created Snaper, hoping she would teach you to be strong or maybe hoping she would protect you. You may think that she failed you, but that's another session. The difference with Snaper is, I don't believe she was one of your personalities."

"Who was she then? Was she real?"

"No, a hallucination; I'm fairly certain. You created her outside of yourself somehow."

"I don't understand."

"You saw her, you heard her, but she was not real."

"So, I'm so fucked up that I created mini-me's and ghosts?" She was angry now… and scared. Tears were building in her eyes. When Dalton released her hand and put his arm around her, she lost it.

They waited through her hysteria and her sobs. As she calmed, he said, "I loved those mini-me's… remember?"

He almost got a smile… almost.

Rain remained silent, so Echo went on. "Sage appeared when your mom died. She couldn't be from within you; she couldn't be like you. She came from your need to be needed and distracted… consumed. You needed an outside force to hold and care for. It was that nurturing that kept you going and gave you what you needed to survive. Sage may have been the one that helped you the most. If you could have come to the realization she wasn't real, but most hallucinations don't change. They stay the same as when they were created; the same age, the same look. But Sage didn't; she grew like a normal child for you. That hampered your ability to see reality."

"I am really, really sick, aren't I?"

"You were maybe, but your getting better now."

"Dalton, you should go." Rain said, avoiding his eyes. "You don't need to see me like this. I can only hurt you."

"I can't go, I won't go and the only thing that can hurt me is if I have to live without you."

"Why?" She began to cry again. "Why do you want to be with me; with this sick thing that I am."

"All of you, the mini-me's and the imaginary family… all good. There is not a one that I would not like. You didn't create bad things, bad people; you…" He was choking up and his words drifted off, but he pulled her tighter against him.

"I love you Jessie Dalton Jentaske… all three of you. Thank you for loving me back, but I think that makes you crazier than me."

Echo sighed… content, but this session was over.

Chapter 26

SHE DARE NOT THINK. IF she did she would run and hide... maybe forever. She needed to fill her life with mind blinding distractions and leave the reality of life to Echo.

She put the breath mint in her mouth and dove under the covers. His soft toy slipped between her lips, now hot from the mint.

"Oh my, Rain; what are you doing?"

"If you don't know, I'd better work harder."

He chuckled saying, "No, no... I mean why does it feel so hot?"

"Is it a good feeling or a bad feeling?" she asked, a little afraid of the answer.

"It's amazing, but what is it?"

She put another one in her mouth and went back to work for he was not boasting a full hard erection. She did not release him until his pleasure was complete and his erection was melting in her mouth.

"What was that?" he asked, as he pulled her up into his arms.

"Just a mint."

"Just a mint?"

"Yes."

"Show me."

She handed him the Listerine paper mints.

"This is what you put in your mouth; this and nothing more?"

"Yes."

"Okay good. Now it's my turn." He headed down between her legs with a grin.

"Oh, I don't know." She'd only heard about them, she'd never used them… Oohhh, you are right; it's very good." She purred.

He stopped and looked up at her. "You like it, huh?"

"Oh yes, I like it; more… give me more."

Orgasm complete, he rises up and she looked at his proturding erection. She motioned with her finger, "Come here; we musn't waste a minute getting that thing some place warm."

In moments, another shared orgasm was vibrating through their bodies.

****

She lay awake long after Dalton had drifted off; her mind drifting and spinning… *God how she loved this man; Jessie Dalton Jentaske. Jessie and Breeze… she tried to draw their wild kinkyness into her, but it was still too strange. It was still her sister. Ember and Task, the romancing cowboy; also still her sister. He would always be Dalton to her, but she wanted to have all of him including the kinky and the cowboy. Would it come in time? Would she ever be one with her sisters?*

The mint tonight; it was an amazing inhancement, but scary, as she'd not only never done that before… she'd never done anything remotely like it before. Dalton was her fir… Holy Crap!!! My first? All those men that Breeze had been with… that was me. I can't… this is too much.

And River, why did he let me do this? He must have known I was sick. Why didn't he try to get me help? The stories of my sisters dieing… was that him trying to help me be free of them? It's all so confusing.

It was already breaking light when she finally drifted off. He let her sleep. At 11:00 he brought her coffee and a breadfast buritto.

"Time to get ready; we see Echo at 1:00." He said, setting the tray down and kissing her cheek.

****

"You know it's amazing how the personalities, the hallucinations and you, all co-exist; the way you cross communicate and have lives that are independent and intertwine." Echo told her. "There is one more thing we have to bring into the equation... River."

"My brother; why?"

"Because he's not real either."

"That's impossible."

"You are an only child. Do you remember what you told me about River when you first came to me?"

"What do you mean?"

"It was the first time you actually saw your father attack your mother. You said, *"Where's my brother? My brother should be here like the big brothers on TV that help and protect their little sisters and brothers."* You were 4. I think that's when you created River. The first two sisters were already a work in progress."

"But River..."

"I think that somehow you had River bring them all to you; the personalities and the hallucinations. That way, if he brought them, you did not have to take responsibility if they were bad, did bad things, made mistakes... did not do what you needed them to do."

"He is my big brother. He was our protector; the big brother I always wanted in another life, but I don't believe in reincarnation, so that is a contradiction of facts. Oh my god; I did create him. Is he me or my imagination?"

"He's an hallucination. He was never one of your personalities, but your hallucination of him came from inside you, like an imaginary friend fits the childs need for a playmate."

Dalton and Echo waited out the long silence as she processed it all and finally she said, "I think I understand... a little." She turned to Dalton. "Does that make sense to you?"

"Yes, I think it does."

"You separated each life and blocked information to keep yourself separate, but then you released what ever you needed or wanted to know through River. That way you didn't have to process it or accept it as your own. When they weren't good for you or they weren't necessary anymore, River killed them. But they aren't gone

Rain; they haven't really died. They are still within you in a way. The strongest part of each of them that you needed, is in you now. Those things have always been in you, but you called on your sisters to bring it to the surface; you just didn't know it. You have a form of schizophrenia, you are delusional at times, you have very rare visual as well as auditory hallucinations and a multiple personality disorder. Sometimes you are them through the personality disorder and what they do is really you and sometimes you see them as hallucinations and what they do is not real... more like symbolic. You may be them or you may be with them or you may be the observer as they play out their part, but you deny it all in your consious mind."

"I can't do this anymore now." she said. "I need to go."

"Rain please, we'll wait for you to catch up. Try to relax. Do you want to lie down?"

"No... no more. I have to go."

"Tomorrow then. You will think about all this, but I want you to rest mostly. I'll give Dalton a seditive for you in case you can't sleep. A sleep deprived mind will never survive this."

****

She ate with Dalton, but she wasn't hungry. They watched a movie, but she never saw it or heard a word. She showered, but she didn't remember doing it and she slept without the medication.

And then Session 14...

"Who really killed my sisters?"

"I believe it was River; remember we talked about that."

"Does that mean I am a murderer?"

"No, but we do need more answers. He told you where they were and how they died, but you need to know why. You have to pull him back, talk to him and find out whats missing."

"You want me to talk to River now... my not-real brother? Now? Here in front of you both?"

"I want you to lay down and close your eyes. I want you to relax and think about him and just let your mind flow. When you're ready, tell us what he said."

"I'll try." She got up and moved to the other couch. "Wouldn't it be better if you hypnotized me?"

"Not if we can do it without."

She lay silently for a long time. She seemed to be asleep when she began talking.

"Snaper was in the trees and her killer... I can't see him, but he's sad. He told her that she ruined everything and she wasn't useful anymore. He said he was sorry, but that now she would rest."

Silence again and they waited... she spoke again.

"I love you." He whispered; pain and sadness in his voice. "You have done well; you have offered possibilities for thought." Now rest Havannah." Without pausing she said, "He told Blaze that she'd also done well; that her work was done. He said, "You are precious, you are loved and now you will rest." He cried... he cried when he killed each of them."

Rain was crying now, but remained asleep. Then slowly her sobs subsided and she lay quiet. An hour passed and they waited.

Rain's voice startled them... "He said Sage helped as a child, but he'd waited long enough for her to be helpful again. He said that now she just caused apprehension; that she was falling into a self-made pit, overcast with disaster and before the emnity got too great, it had to end. It's like his heart was being torn out of him. He loves them and still he kills them."

Silence.

"You learned love and you brought it into the essence, but now you're in the way."

Echo and Dalton looked at each other. This was not Rain's voice; then who's? The killer? River maybe? They waited.

"The doors have to open and there can be no door stops to trip over. I'm sorry, but you will rest now." The voice was a man's voice and it was racked with pain and sorrow. Were those the words he'd spoken to Ember before he killed her? Dalton and Echo looked at each other, confused... unsure.

Silence again; this time so loud it was deafening as they waited... Until, at last, Rain's voice was heard. "Don't be afraid." That's what he told her. "You have done well Pocahontus, but she can do it now;

she's almost free. It's time for you to rest." He spoke with so much love."

The silence this time had been so long that Dalton stepped out and ordered food, but when it came, Rain was still asleep and they were afraid to wake her. They ate in silence and waited. It was dark when she stretched and sat up. She remembered nothing, so Echo let her listen to the tape.

"That was River's voice." She said. "What do you think it all means?"

"I'm in overload." Dalton said, shaking his head.

"I believe that you called River and he called your sisters; yes, it all came from somewhere deep inside you, but you are all separate just the same.

Since he called them into being, when they finished their work, he had to remove them so that you... the real you, could take what they had given you and claim it as your own."

"But how, if I was Ember..., how did my hallucination kill her without killing me?"

"I need more time to be sure, but for now... two options that I can see; either he is a hallucination, so he can't really kill you, except that sort of theory has been proven to be wrong. If the hallucination is real enough the person can die. So I'm inclined to go with the theory that somehow the personality seperated from you and became a vision within your hallucination. I know it all seems so far fetched, but I don't think this condition has ever been documented before. I believe it was your way of letting go."

"I'm hungry." She proceeded to scarf down over half a large cold pizza, two bread sticks, chocolate cake and 3 sodas. The session was over.

****

A year of sessions had passed... she was afraid that she'd have years more to come. She had found the ability to live her life, most of the time, as though it was all a bad dream far in her past. There were relapses, short lived. There were passing hours of seclusion, memories and reflection, but she lived on...

Rain surprised him with a trip to the mountains. It was snow covered and they had to hike the last mile to the cabin. The road was closed. They covered their backs with everything they could carry and would make another trip the next day. On their walk, they had stopped to watch deer in the distance; a fox that was a little too close for Dalton's comfort and rabbits that caused her concern due to the cold. They unpacked the most needed supplies, made a fire, ate and curled up in front of the fire and made love; then slept like rocks.

In the morning, she slipped out for a short walk in the snow. He was still asleep when she returned. She leaned over and kissed him softly and started the coffee. She removed her cold wet clothes and took a cup and set it by the bed. When she looked at him sleeping, her chest expanded as her heart filled with even more love. She leaned over to kiss his closed eyelids and he reached and pulled her down on top of him. As they thrashed around laughing, she felt his passion growing against her. The next kiss was deep and wet; their tongues in a frenzy.

She nibbled on his neck, his shoulder and a tiny little nipple. She devoured his belly button and slithered on down like a snake until she was teasing the tip of his erection. Spreading his legs she moved down to nibble his derriere' and the smaller, softer toys. He shivered and groaned and the moment she slipped her lips over him... he came.

She felt the spasm of readiness between her thighs. He entered her quickly, hoping to make her cum before he lost his erection... "You are the depth of my passion." She whispered, as she tensed against him deep inside her. She came, trembling beneath him.

They got the rest of the supplies from the truck, they had a snow fight, they built a snowman and now they'd finished dinner and were sitting by the fire, sipping hot chocolate.

He dozed while she slipped into her night gown, lit the candles and turned out the lights. She whispered, "Get naked kind sir; it's time for your massage."

He stood before her, naked.

"Oh my, sir; you must cover that. This is not that kind of place."

He grabbed the blanket and covered himself. She threw him a towel. "This will be enough sir. You needn't over re-act." It was all she could do not to giggle.

"On your back." She ordered. She began at his temple and massaged every inch to his toes, except she carefully avoided his twiching appendage. She sucked erotically on his toes and then, "On your stomach." She ordered.

She began at his toes and worked up to his neck not missing an inch. Now the massage complete she rolled off laying on her back next to him.

"Straddle me as I did you." She ordered. "I missed a spot."

Sitting across her hips with his trinket resting softly on her stomach he asked, "Now what?"

"Scoot up."

He grinned as he moved up, slipping his full blown erection between her lips.

The final touch to the massage begins as he moves in and out of her lips. When he was about to cum he pulled free.

"No." he said, moving back. "I need to be in you." He whispered.

He leaned and kissed her, searching gently the entirety of her mouth with his tongue. He devoured each breast and toyed with her naval. He brought her to the brink with his tongue and then he slipped into her; not just her cave, but her essence, her being... her soul and they were one.

Laying beside her, holding her in wonder... this woman; this broken woman that he loved so much... even her brokenness, her fractured self was treasured, precious, beautiful to him. He looked into her eyes and she could feel his thoughts. She didn't know the words, but she knew the feeling his thoughts portrayed.

"With you there is no yesterday, no tomorrow." He whispered. "Each moment is an infinite perfection of love and passion; pure, strong and undeniable."

Chapter 27

RAIN WENT HOME BY HERSELF to unload some things from the trip and pick up a few things. Dalton insisted she stay with him at least until her therapy was over; forever preferably, he'd said. She could not answer; she did not yet feel the freedom to committ and that worried her a little. She would discuss it sometime with Echo when they were alone. She had to protect Dalton from herself until she was well.

She packed and as she walked towards the door, suitcase in hand, she heard, "It's okay Rain. I love you."

She turned to find River leaning against the door frame behind her. There were tears in his eyes, but he was maintaining. "I will miss you, but I'm excess baggage now."

She knew in her head he wasn't real, but in her heart it was different. She ran to him and threw her arms around his neck. "I love you too. You have been…" The words drifted off into the air as she clung to him.

"You are so strong now; you have all the things you need or you know how to find them. Peace, love, wisdon, strength and maybe even God. There is only one thing left. Can you do it; are you strong enough to take that last step to freedom?"

She stepped back; eyes wide, mouth open, realizing what he wanted; the shock of it vibrating through her body. "You… you want me to kill you?"

"You have no choice. I'm all that stands between you and freedom. You have not seen me in over a year and you have been fine; you must let me go."

"No! No I can't; I won't."

"If I do it myself, you won't be free."

"No… that's not what I want either. Why do you have to die? Can't you just…?"

"Just what my little sister?"

"I don't know; I have to go. Maybe Echo can help us find another way." She didn't wait for an answer; she ran to her car as fast as she could and drove away… and away… and away.

Suddenly she realized she had no idea where she was. She looked around trying to get her bearings. She called Dalton.

"Where are you? I was getting worried and you didn't answer your phone."

"I'm sorry; I got caught up with things at the house and then I went for a drive and lost track of time."

"A drive… alone? Are you alright?"

"Yes, the sound of your voice makes me alright. I needed to think, or I thought I did, and ended up mindlessly driving. I'll be home in an hour; I drove farther than I intended. I'm going to give Echo a quick call and I'll be on my way."

****

"This is Dr. McMasters."

"Echo, this is Rain. Could we move our session up to tomorrow? I hate to ask; I know you have other patients, but…"

"Are you alright? Do we need to meet tonight? What is it?"

"Tomorrw will be fine. I am better than I was earlier and Dalton is waiting for me. I don't want to worry him."

"Tomorrow then. I'll see you at 1:00."

The truth was, Dalton was already worried. If she was calling Echo, something must be wrong. He wished she'd get home. He greeted her at the door with hugs and kisses and made her sit down to dinner. He insisted the dishes would wait and he took her to the couch. Taking her hands in his, he said softly, "Tell me now."

"What?"

"Rain, don't do this. We share everything; we hold back nothing. I am not leaving you."

"I know; that's why you should be spared what ever I can do on my own."

"I don't want to be spared. I know if you had to call Echo, you were scared; I need to know what scared you."

"Are you sure?"

"I thougth we covered all this a long time ago. Don't ever doubt me; nothing has changed and nothing will."

She fidgeted and then looked into his eyes. "At the house today; I saw River. We talked."

"Are you alright?"

"No, he said I had to kill him. I can't do that. I know in my head he's not real, but in my heart I love him. I can't kill those I don't love; how do I kill the brother I do love."

"I don't know babe; this is beyond me. You were right to call Echo. What did she say?"

"Our session is tomorrow at 1:00."

"We'll be there."

They went to bed, he held her... she wept... they slept.

****

Rain had given Dalton a few errands to keep him busy for about an hour. "I hate to ask, but I know I'm not going to feel like doing it after the session and I hate leaving things till the last minute."

"I don't want to leave you." He said feeling apprehensive.

"You'll grow to hate me for it, but I'm anal about getting that to-do list done."

She **was** sort of anal, but today it was just because she needed a few minutes with Echo alone.

"But I should be here with you."

191

"The first little while is chit chat anyway and then we start with the lighter stuff. By the time we get to the serious part of the session, you'll be back."

"You're right; I'm being over cautious."

Tears filled her eyes.

"Rain what...?"

"I'm sorry. Dalton, I'm sorry."

"For what?"

"The errands... they're just an excuse."

"For what?" He was pulling her to him now.

"I need to discuss something with Echo alone for a few minutes. I should have just told you; I'm sorry. I thought a little deception... no big deal, but it is a big deal. It twisted in my gut, not being honest with you."

"Do you know how much I love you for that; how much that means to me?"

"I know how much it would mean to me, but now I'm hating that I need this time."

"Don't, you will talk to me about whatever it is when your ready. I don't believe you will hold back once you've talked it through with Echo and understand it better yourself."

"God I love you." She said, tightening her grip on him.

He pulled back enough to slip a finger under her chin and tip her face up to his. He kissed her, "We'd better get going."

****

He dropped her off with a kiss and an... "I'll see you in a few."

Echo handed her a cup of tea. "Ready?"

"Eager."

"Last night...?"

"Yes, I've been staying with Dalton since... since we realized what was wrong with me. He wants me to move in with him. He said at least until the therapy is complete, but he says he really wants long term... like maybe forever."

"And that's a problem for you?"

"I have this underlying fear that I'm not free to make that commitment. I want to; I want forever with him, so why am I still afraid? I should feel nothing but relief and joy."

"A forever commitment is a fearful thing for all of us, not just you and not just people with... problems. It's normal."

"It's not that kind of fear. I get that, but this is different. It's like I still have something in me that keeps me from having full control; from being free."

"River." Echo said, matter of fact.

"What?"

"We still have to deal with River."

"Oh God... how did you know? Did Dalton?"

"What... what is it?" Echo said, concerned. "Has something happened?"

"You think River is keeping me from Dalton?"

"In a way, maybe. I don't have any other explanation for your fear... why is that so...?"

"River is the reason I called you last night."

"What happened?"

"I went by the house to drop off some things from our trip and pick up a few things to take to Daltons. When I was leaving, River showed up."

"What happened?"

"I didn't know he was there until I heard him say, "*It's okay; I love you.*" I didn't know what he meant. I know he's not real; my head knows he's not real, but my heart loves him... he's my brother, my protector. Did you know he'd come back to me?"

"No, I didn't know, but since he hadn't died I thought it possible. After about 6 months, I made the mistake of thinking that if he hadn't shown up by then, he wasn't going to. I'm sorry. Did he say anything else?"

"That I had everything I needed now, to be free and stand on my own. He said that the only thing between the broken me and freedom was him. He said I had to kill him. I love him; I can't kill him. You have to help me find another way."

"This should have crossed my mind, but it hasn't. I'm sorry Rain. River needs to not exist for you anymore; that's true. You need to let him go, but I'm afraid I haven't given enough thought as to how. This is my failure. You must know deep inside you that his death is the only way, but I agree… for you to kill him is not the right mode."

"I don't want him to die."

"But you need him to die." They both turned to Dalton, who had come in silently and had been standing just inside the door for the last few minutes.

"Echo's right Rain; you do need him to die."

"I can't kill him."

"Of course not. That's not what we're saying." Dalton was at her side now and holding her; she was trembling.

"We will find the answer." Echo assured her. "Dalton, can I get you some tea?"

"No thank you; I'm fine."

"Rain? A refill?"

"Yes please."

They sat in silence while she tended to the tea; all of their minds spinning… with nothing. The question was there, flashing in big bold letters, but no soultions were within reach of their thoughts.

"Dalton, go over to the recliner and lie back, relax and try to sleep. See what might come to mind. Rain, the couch, get comfortable; you know the routine. Just wait to see if your subconscious mind will take over; then tell us what it says."

They both did as they were told and Echo too leaned back and tried to relax… and wait. Two hours passed, Dalton appeared to be in a fairly deep sleep. Rain was dozing lightly by the sound of her breathing. Echo was nearly asleep herself when she heard, *"Remember, death shall not prevail for even in death, life and love remain."* It was a whisper and she didn't catch it all, but as Rain repeated it three or four times, it became clear. She'd heard it before, but where? There was silence again. Echo thought maybe, if Rain said it now, she might be the one she heard it from before. She began going over her notes.

Dalton woke and she explained what had happened and what she was doing. She was three hours into her notes when she found it. By now Rain was sitting up too.

"It was River who said that to you after Blaze died; to comfort you. Maybe he was saying those words to you again, to comfort you over his death."

"He's not dead."

"He's preparing you."

Dalton sat captivated by these two women, sitting there talking about him like he was real instead of a hallucination. It made him realize just how real he must be to Rain. His heart broke for her. She was going to have to lose the brother she loved. Her loss would be as real as if **he** was real.

****

There was a large section of woods at the base of the mountain just outside of town. It covered nearly three square miles. There were hiking paths and dirt roads weaving all over it. It had many names. The official one was "Tolden Memorial Park". The land was donated by the Tolden family when the old man died. It was also called "Bears Den" by those who love to camp and fish near the small pond at the north end. Others called it "Jogger's Ridge" and still others called it "VD Central", for it was well known for "Hooker" traffic. The high school kids used it for a "Lover's Lane" as well.

In the last three months there had been 5 murders there. They were all men in their early 30's, good looking and they all had ejaculated semen just before death. Two were married; three were single. They were happening in all different parts of the woods and they had no leads.

It was River's favorite place to run since he'd returned to her life. "A man has to keep in shape." He'd tell Rain. Since the first murder, she had asked him to find a different place and he promised he would, but she didn't know if he had.

Rain had mentioned this to Echo in an earlier session. Now, she wondered what a hallucination did when it was not in the presence of the one hallucinating. Did River run in the woods or did he just wait for her to see him again and then say he did it?

Echo decided she must be tired or desperate for she had thought about that same question. Her mind was acting crazier than her patients.

****

Rain had spent the night at her own home, much against Dalton's wishes. She insisted she had to do this alone. She hoped the answer would come to her in her home, where all her sickness began; where River may be more likely to appear.

"I'm going out for a run." River had called into her room as he ran past.

"Wait, it's still dark." But he was already gone.

She had slept in her clothes and didn't bother to change when she decided to join him; it seemed the only way to get to talk to him… to find an answer.

When she parked the sun wasn't up yet. The fullness of darkness had faded only slightly, so that she could see without a flashlight if she was careful. She had no idea which trail he'd taken, so she just took a chance on a gut feeling and headed down one.

She heard a scream, a woman she was sure. It stopped and she could hear yelling… she ran towards it. Someone needed help. She saw the tent, the fire, the man struggling beneath another man and River running towards them.

She froze; immobilized, powerless to speak or move… her eyes locked on the men fighting and the knift that glittered in the fire-light. The man swung his hand back raising the knife high and in so doing, caught River in the throat as he leaned over them, trying to stop the man with the knife.

Rain gasped and her hand flew to her mouth to muffle it as she watched the knife pounding down over the man on the ground… over and over as River dropped to the ground, holding his throat.

The man ran, he was cursing. She pulled her phone, dialing 911 as she ran to her brother's side.

His neck was bleeding heavily and his words gurgled as he said, "It's okay; I will rest." And he was gone.

She was sitting there crying, holding her brother as the police and ambulances pulled up. They couldn't see River of course and it took a moment for her to realize that. She remained kneeled on the ground, holding his head, next to the body of the other man. Her tears stopped when they began to ask questions, but she refused to move. They assumed she was in shock and wrapped a blanket around her shoulders and let her stay where she was.

"Is there anyone we can call for you?" She gave them Dalton's number. He'd be panicked, but he'd know she was alright and he would come.

"Can you tell us what happened?"

She began to speak mechanically, "I was just going for an early walk and I heard a woman screem. When I got closer, I saw the tent, the fire and a man hovering over the man on the ground with a knife. I didn't see the woman."

They had found her inside the tent with three stab wounds, but she was alive... barely. The ambulance had already taken her away. "He just kept stabbing him and then he ran off cursing."

"Did you get a good look at him?"

"I got a long look at him, but not a good one; it was dark."

"Tell us what you can."

"He was wearing dark clothes, black I think, and I think black gloves because I didn't see a lighter color holding the knife. If it was his skin it should have been lighter, like skin on his face."

"Did you see his face?"

"No, he never turned my way. I don't think he knew I was here. I'd probably be dead too if he'd seen me."

"You could be right."

"Anything else you can tell us?"

"Just that he had a big nose. I was looking at him from the side, so I could see his nose was exceptionally large."

She heard them speaking among themselves. "I'll bet he didn't know the woman was here. This guy fits the M.O.; 36, good looking and stabbed to death. I think the woman was a surprise and because of it the guy was cheated out of his semen and that's why he was pissed off."

"But if he didn't know she was here, why would he be scared off?"

"A hunch, a feeling he was being watched. Maybe he heard a noise. Who the hell knows."

"That's what I'd bet my money on. He just spooked." Another detective agreed.

Dalton was here running towards her. "Oh my God baby; what the hell?" His arms were around her and that's all that mattered.

He looked at the body in front of her and up at the officer. "Can I take her home now?"

"I think that'd be alright, but we'll need her to come in tomorrow and make an official statement." He handed Dalton a card with the information on it. "And stop tracking up our crime sceene."

"I'll bring her down; will late afternoon be alright."

"Morning sir, in the morning; by noon."

"Alright."

He started to lift her. "Dalton, wait; I need just a minute."

He looked at her strange, stopped and watched her. She looked down at her lap and placed her hands there. She whispered something and then... what? No... she didn't just kiss the air. She looked up at him as he realized she'd just said good-bye to her brother. River was dead.

"I'm ready now." She whispered.

He helped her up and took her to the truck. As she looked back, her brother's body was gone. They rode in silence, but at home, as he held her in bed she said, "Thank you."

"For...?"

"For not asking, but I'm going to tell you."

"You read my mind too?"

"God I hope so."

He kissed her and snuggled her back in his arms, her hand resting on his chest.

"It was River."

"I know. What happened?"

"He got there before I did. He was trying to help the man being stabbed. When the killer swung the knife back, it caught River in the throat. He bled to death in my arms."

"Oh Rain... I'm so sorry. I should have been there."

"No, you shouldn't; I had to do this alone. Before he died he said, "It's okay; I will rest. It was what he said about all my sisters when they died. He said they were resting now."

Dalton sat up, took her shoulders and turned her to him. Looking into her eyes he said, "And it is okay, isn't it? He freed you of your final bond."

"I think so."

They made gentle, sweet, terder love and drifted off to sleep.

****

He took her to the station and she gave them her statement. While there they learned that the wife had regained consciousness and told them that her husband had gone out to revive the fire for coffee. A man came in the tent. She thought it was her husband and when she realized it wasn't she screamed. He stabbed her as her husband came in the tent. That's all she said before she passed out again.

"I'm afraid she died about three hours later." The officer told them.

They went straight to Dr. McMaster's office.

"River died last night."

"How are you handling it?"

"Pretty well, thanks to Dalton."

"How did he die?"

She told her the whole story and all the appropriate things of comfort were spoken.

Rain, and even Dalton, had felt like River had written the scenario of his death in order to let Rain off the hook. Now, listening to the story again, Dalton realized that was not possible. He was Rain's hallucination; it had to come from her. He looked over at Echo knowing she was thinking the same thing.

199

They both realized, if Rain considered that fact, she may resume the guilt of his death. They would remain silent and deal with it… if and when it happened.

"I'll want to see you weekly for the next month and if all is well, once a month for three months and then every three months for a year."

"Why, do you think I will relapse somehow?"

I don't, but we have to be sure and… if for no other reason than I want to keep updated on your happy life." she grinned.

"What if they come back?"

"That's highly unlikely."

"What if new ones come?"

"With your new state of mind and your new life, that too is highly unlikely, but we will deal with it if it happens. If they come back, don't be afraid to live in their shoes; you lived through them and they will always live through you."

"And new ones?"

"Just remember, you're the boss now; you're in control."

Epilogue

EIGHTEEN MONTHS LATER AND THE story is direct from Rain's point of view… We're going to church now and Dalton and I are both studying with Quake. He was back to work and so was I… part time.

Rain Hardecky and Jessie Dalton Jentaske…; it was too soon for 'Happily Ever After', but "happy" we were, every day… all the time.

Sometimes I struggled with the fear of getting sick again, but mostly I just stumbled in the brightness of the colors of the happiness, that this man I loved brought me, as I lingered through one day and on to the next.

Then I got an idea… a little spice I'd never been brave enough to tackle. A co-worker had a brother who was a dog catcher and he was happy to lend his services. I would see just how well Dalton fell into the fantasy… with me. I sent him his costume… Tramp and told him to meet me at the corner of Pecos and Jarvice at 7:00 pm… and be in character. I made a lovely cocker spanial if I do say so myself.

I waited on the sidewalk on all fours. At 7:00 pm sharp, Tramp came loping around the corner barking. Well, on all fours loping might be a bit of an exaggeration. The dog catcher grabbed me and put me in the back of the truck and drove slowly away with Tramp chasing along behind.

It was only a half a block to the dog catchers house where he'd lock me in a cage in his front yard. Well not really lock… Tramp did not disappointment me as he opened that cage with his teeth and we loped off… okay not lope, but it was more than sauntered.

To my surprise, there was a taxi on the street near by and it stopped in front of us. The driver got out and opened the back door. Tramp crawled in on all fours and then back out. With a front leg, he motioned me to get in first. '*OOhhhh… Tramp the gentleman.*' We were dropped off on a corner I did not recognize. He led me around back to the alley and walked two businesses down and stood barking at the back door. I was mesmerized and curious. What was he doing?

The door opened and a man in an apron came out with a small table and two chairs. He began to speak in an Italian accent and he spoke the words right out of the movie. He served spaghetti and wine… no bread sticks or salad. We sucked spaghetti just like Lady and the Tramp. I can't begin to explain how amazing all this felt. Then we were back in the taxi and home making love in our costumes doggy style.

"*Breeze was a genius,*" I thought. "*I have to keep doing this now and then.*"

When I woke in the morning, I heard whimpering and whining; there were 6 little Lady and the Tramp puppies in a basket next to my bed. I didn't get to keep them; they were on loan from a pet store owned by a friend of his.

After breakfast we played with our guests the rest of the day, but they were being picked up at 3:00. When they were gone and we were snuggled in front of the fire, he whispered, "Thank you for the most beautiful surprise ever. You made our other fantasies come together with fantasies of our own." He said lovingly.

"First… you made the fantasy as wonderful as it was; all I did was push the start button. It is I who should be thanking you. Second… thank you for thinking of the fantasies with Breeze as ours."

"They are ours; it was you… and I want you to think about them until you feel the sensations and emotions that we shared back then. I know you can do it… we are one."

Words were gone, the kisses were deep and wet, the touches firm and exciting, the words erotic and sensuous… our bodies slamming together, sensations shooting to all the right places, tensions building higher and higher until the explosions of orgasms filled us with heavenly pleasures. There were butterfly kisses and gentle caresses in the afterglow and warm sweet words of love in the aftermath.

****

He woke at 3:00 am; he couldn't sleep. He began to nibble on her shoulders. She wiggled a bit and with a semi-stretch she opened her eyes and looked over her shoulder at him.

"I'm sorry; I couldn't sleep." He said a little pathetically.

"Can I share your insomnia for a while." She asked.

"I thougt you'd never ask." He was grinning now.

"What's keeping you awake? Can I help? A massage maybe."

"I wake you up in the middle of the night and you offer me a massage. How did I get so lucky?"

"Do you want one?"

"No… what I really want is for you to take the final test." He said.

"The final test?"

"Of freedom."

"Alright… what…?" she said hesitantly.

"Will you marry me?"

"Do you think I'm ready?"

"That has to come from you. I want to marry you ready or not."

"You think it was River holding me back. How did you know?"

"How did I know that it was River that kept you from… I didn't. Not for sure."

"I hope our knowing of each other never changes." She said softly.

"We'll never let it change… so, will you marry me?"

"Yes…yes… I will marry you and I will love you past the death bed to the end of eternity."

****

I was nearly 40 when I discovered I was 8 weeks pregnant. I was scared at first and didn't know how to tell him, but I figured it out. I went and bought the book and the movie… Lady and the Tramp. I left the book on the bed open to the part where the baby came in and I fast forwarded the movie to where she told him she was pregnant. I went to bed first and turned my back to his side, pretending I'd fallen asleep reading and left the movie on pause.

He picked up the book as he crawled into bed. "Reading a reminder of our escapades babe?" he said as he kissed my shoulder. "That Tramp sure knew how to protect his baby and I know how to attack mine." He was getting playful and so was I… it was doggy style again. As he flopped down beside me, I pushed play.

He watched. "What is this Lady… are you hinting for more?" He was grinning.

"I am hinting, but not for more."

He turned to his side facing me and lay his hand on my stomach. "For what then?" He asked.

I lay my hand over his on my belly. "Will you still want me when my body changes?" I was looking at our hands.

"Changes? What are you…" Light bulb!! "Oh… oh; you mean your… we're… pregnant?"

"Yes." I grinned. "Are you happy?"

"Give me a girl; I want another you around… or a boy if you must."

"And when I'm fat and have stretch marks and saggy tits and…?" My eyes were filled with tears. I hadn't thought about that part until just now.

"Can I kiss them when they get that way?"

"Uh huh."

"Then on with it; let's have a baby."

We were all kisses and hugs and plans… until exhausted, we fell asleep. Well, he fell asleep and I lay awake with a grin thinking, *"Now that we're having a baby, I wonder if he'd like a Mary Poppin's fantasy?"*

The next day, when he came home from work, he held in his arms our very own "Lady and the Tramp".

****

Yes, it's true… Death shall not prevail, for even in death, life and love remain.

More Books by This Author

A 13-book series based on a true story called…
Forbidden Gardens in the Diary of a Lifetime

Subtitles
The Cowboy and the Cougar
And Then He Was Gone
Written in Stone
Step By Step
Sex, Dreamscapes and Love Without Mercy
Encounters, Memories and Rendezvous'
The Clouds of My Fantasies
To Live is to Love Though Love Be
Heaven or Love Be Hell
Rainbows of Pleasure… Flavors of Passion
Desperate Distractions
I Hear the Accuser Roar
The Birth of Acceptance

****

A Book of Poetry
Scattered Thoughts in the Clouds of My Fantacies

****

Children's Book's
Cocoa and Rascal
Little Bears Extrodinaire
&
Sammy's Nightmare

****

Romantic, Erotic, Graphic Thriller (5-book Series)
The Tide of Dark Red Blood
Paradise Lost in the Tide of Dark Red Blood
The Mazes of Life in Paradise Flow
with Dark Red Blood
The Tide of Dark Red Blood Flows Against
the Rainbows of Love in Paradise
The Tide of Dark Red Blood the Beginning of the End

About the Author

 BORN IN SO. DAK. MARRIED military and moved around. 18 yrs. in AZ. 30 yrs. In New Mexico. Mother of 3, grandmother of 4, great grandmother of 7. Married x2 – Totally in love x5. Hopeless romantic. Love hiking in the wilderness. Collect artifacts and bones. Life excites me and I can't wait to see whats around the corner of my life. I have a 5 book series and 4 childrens books I hope to have you publish in the next 4 or 5 years. I got my 1st tattoo at 66. I now have 62, I think. They tell my story.

Printed in the USA
CPSIA information can be obtained
at www.ICGtesting.com
CBHW030856031024
15215CB00091B/1682

9 781637 847091